Eyeshine

Cy Wyss

Nighttime Dog Press, LLC
P.O. Box 816
Zionsville, IN 46077
http://www.nighttimedogpress.com

Contents

Spring Festival

People called Brooke Annabeth Taylor "PJ," which stood not for pajamas but for Peeping Jane. She'd been a photographer and reporter for as long as the town could remember—at least since grade school—and her reportage was known for the most candid and impossible photos, like Peter Parker's but from nearer the ground. Her job was made more difficult by her moniker because once people found out what it was, they shied away and wouldn't tell her the secrets that are a reporter's stock-in-trade. As she got older, it got harder and harder to convince anyone to give her a story. Now, at thirty, she was no longer "kitten cute" and able to wile her way easily into subjects' confidence. Still, she managed to find a way. With her penetrating amber eyes and easy smile, people found her disarming. She loved her relationship as a freelance reporter with the town's paper, and all the vagaries that life entails, such as being a night owl and an absolute bulldog for the truth. If she could have chosen her own moniker, it would have likely combined these: Owl Dog. It was particularly inappropriate, however, because she turned not into a bird or canine every night, but into a cat.

She had been a black tabby from sundown to sunup since shortly after puberty. She often wondered why other people didn't morph into alternate beings for the dark hours, but was admonished very early on by a loving mother to never, never, ever speak a word of it to anyone. PJ liked to think that was because her mother had a similar power and had suffered, but it could have been due solely to the woman's intelligence and prudence.

PJ's father had died when she was ten. The man was a scientist, an absent-minded chemist, and PJ was of two minds about his awareness. On the one hand, his cleverness meant surely he wouldn't have been fooled by a mere wife, no matter how adept at deception; on the other hand, his absent-mindedness meant sometimes he forgot to wear shoes. So it wasn't a stretch to think he might have no inkling about the bizarreness of his wife or daughter.

At sixteen, with PJ in limbo between childhood and womanhood, her mother suffered a tragic and debilitating stroke that took her life within months. PJ then moved in with her much older brother and his family. By then, she had become as adept as her mother at hiding her talent, in spite of the fact her brother was an FBI agent by that time, at twenty-nine, and extraordinarily difficult to deceive. It helped that after he witnessed firsthand the transformation from girl to cat, he immediately went into a long-lasting shock that consisted of utter denial. Instead of considering how her unique power could assist him in his life of crime fighting, he grounded her for a month and kept her largely confined to her room, especially after sundown.

PJ forgave Robert for locking her up, only because of her natural optimism and sense of personal grandeur. Honestly, grudges were beneath her, as were most things mere mono-modal humans did. She focused on her schoolwork and got all A's that semester. Much later she discovered her brother had to take a polygraph test every year he was employed with the all-knowing government agency. PJ realized Robert had so thoroughly put the image of his sister becoming a black tabby cat out of his mind that he had convinced himself it wasn't even a hallucination—it simply hadn't existed at all. There's no need to lie if you're a true believer, and that was the most effective path for a forced deceiver. So PJ kept her secret, and Robert kept his job.

Fourteen years later, PJ was irrevocably known as Peeping Jane and Robert had traveled the country and come back in his forties to set up a one-man field office in Mayhap, Indiana. One day, PJ was out with her best friends Clara Goodwind and Vicky Donnerweise at the Mayhap Spring Festival when the sun dipped low on the horizon, threatening to bring the stars closer and the day to an end.

"PJ, why do you always leave just when things are getting interesting?" Clara asked.

She was a buxom woman with big hazel eyes and bright red hair. Her wardrobe favored items with cats in evidence or implied by pithy sayings, such as "Meow Happens," which her pink tube top currently sported. The woman was Taft County's prime cat rescuer, with a warren of dedicated chicken-wire pens covering her backyard and a full-time feeding schedule. When she wasn't volunteering at the county's humane shelter, she was ensconced in a network of gossips centered at the Mayhap Memorial Library. Clara was an assistant librarian but party to all the good stories the town could provide. PJ found her an invaluable source. If it happened, or was going to happen, Clara knew about it and would talk.

Vicky stood with arms akimbo and watched PJ inhale an elephant ear. She was a striking woman with hair even blacker than PJ's and blue eyes where PJ's were yellow. Vicky was tall and muscular, like a man, but lither and hourglass-shaped inside the bulky kit she wore for law enforcement. She was one of Taft County's deputies, second in their force only to Sheriff Curtis Denning, to whom she happened to be married.

"Land's sake, PJ, how do you eat like that? You know I'm active all day, but I can't eat three of those things without being ten pounds fatter tomorrow. Do you just stay up all night on the treadmill or what?"

A loud cry of enjoyment crescendoed from the fairway before PJ could answer, which was just as well since her mouth was filled with fried dough and she wouldn't have gotten more than a grunt or two out. She didn't have the heart to enlighten her friend. Every night, indeed, she ran the treadmill of being feline. She wandered miles in the summertime, searched every nook and cranny of the county, chased rodents and vermin, and napped only fitfully and with one eye open under the shifting moon.

She popped the last of the ear into her mouth and said, "It's genetics. Some people are luckier than others."

Vicky and Clara groaned.

Clara adjusted her pink-rimmed glasses and slurped her sno-cone. "At least I managed to keep myself to just one Devil Dog. And sno-cones have no calories after noon—everyone knows that." Clara was constantly watching her figure, which didn't seem to keep her from growing more buxom by the year. At the rate she was going, she would be a round octogenarian with a radiant smile in fifty years. PJ thought things could be worse.

"So you two coming two weeks from today or what?" Vicky said.

She was having a cookout, a common occurrence in the warmer months, and the Taylors and Goodwinds were regular fixtures. Everyone knew the cookouts were as much a bid to stuff the people of Taft County with reasons why the Denning clan should hold on to the sheriff-hood for the indefinite future, but everyone came anyway. Vicky's ribs were legendary, and Curtis's beer was as tasty and free flowing as anyone's ever was. Today was Saturday, and two weeks from today was going to be the first big Donnerweise-Denning BBQ of the season.

"Yeah, I'll be there," PJ said. "At least until sunset."

Vicky rolled her eyes. "Because you turn into a pumpkin at sunset, right? We'll never get to see nighttime you. Isn't Doc Fred helping you with that?"

Doctor Fred Norton was Mayhap's most celebrated, and only, psychiatrist. Apparently he was a third cousin twice removed to the iconic Oprah Winfrey and had once listened to her problems with aplomb, inspiring her to go on and listen eternally to others. He was given a brief mention in a book of hers, which was now out-of-print. For Mayhap, that was all it took to secure one's place in the annals of town history. He even had a special shelf in the library to display his pamphlets on the pluses of positive putation, despite the brochures containing more than their fair share of buzz non-words.

PJ's cover story for disappearing every evening, no matter the weather or event, was a rare and debilitating overreaction to darkness. Everyone thought she ran home to sit in a bright room under full-spectrum lights so she could make it through the dark hours with her psyche intact, her odd and entrenched phobia notwithstanding. Doc Fred made a perfect corroborator. His acute sense of professional delicacy meant he could never confirm nor deny PJ's hints that he was treating her without success for her illness. Perhaps he had spent the last decades sketching her case study, which would no doubt be picked up by the professional societies should it ever come to a positive conclusion.

"Sorry," PJ said to Vicky, "I'm not going to talk about it."

"Oh, right. Shrink's privilege and all that."

"Well, get going," Clara said. "I don't want to have to carry around any pumpkins your size after dark, if you turn into one."

"Alrighty. Toodles, people."

2

Thieves

PJ checked her watch. She had just over fifteen minutes to get home be-fore sunset. The festival was in Mayhap's Central Park, which was only five blocks from her home in Stoker Hills. Every town, no matter how af-fluent, has its less desirable parts, and Mayhap was no exception. Just south of downtown was a trailer park, hidden in the dead-end Lunar Lane and called Stoker Hills. It was about twenty plots, small, with the usual assortment of glorified tin cans and corrugated metal that Mayhap's less fortunate called home. PJ flattered herself that she didn't have to live there—she had a small but workable inheritance from her late parents—but she chose to live among the welfare and working classes. She used to say, "White trash? I fit right in." Nowadays, with the growing foment against the haves in America, she saw things differently. She had a ton of friends in the Hills and didn't like to see them belittle themselves. You didn't need money to be a star, live the American dream, or get yourself and your kids a decent education. Stoker Hills was proof of that, and PJ reminded everyone of that every chance she got. Her latest mantra was, "Salt of the Earth? I fit right in."

PJ passed through the park gates and under trees until she hit the road south of Main Street and took to the cobblestones. Above her, the sky was indigo, speckled with gray clouds. It was the rainy season and had lately been living up to its reputation, but this particular evening the spring festival had gotten a break. It wasn't raining, and none of the fluffy clouds looked threatening enough to ruin the fun.

As PJ passed Main Street, she looked down its length. Mayhap was famous for its Main Street. American flags and budding flowers hung from the lampposts. Along the cobblestone-lined street, midcentury architecture shone in the form of brick buildings, columned white-washed facades, and painted white fences. It was a snapshot of a stereotype, a throwback to a more innocent time. PJ loved her town. Main Street never failed to give her a warm feeling.

She passed the bank and the Dairy Queen and headed past Second Street to where First Avenue turned into Lunar Lane. As she neared the Stoker Hills gates, she encountered a small black cat. She stopped briefly to look at him. He was still a kitten and couldn't have been more than four months old. He had bright yellow eyes, as bright as PJs, one of which was seeping gooey liquid.

"Hey there, little fella," she said.

The kitten was sitting under a tree next to the sidewalk and simply stared at her. He made no movement to run away.

PJ leaned down toward him. The kitten stood up and backed away several steps, still staring intently into her eyes.

"Easy, there. You know, I think you might have an eye infection."

The kitten was on the verge of running away.

"I can't stop now, but if you find me tomorrow, we can get that fixed."

Amber-colored eyes studied PJ carefully, as if trying to understand her words. PJ knew she couldn't successfully communicate with animals in human form. Her soothing tone would put anyone at ease, but of course the kitten didn't understand what she was saying. She checked her watch again. She had to keep going. She could only hope she'd catch sight of the kitten again and be able to help him.

"Bye, little guy," she said and hurried up Lunar Lane through the open iron gate marking Stoker Hills.

The sky was nearly navy by the time she made it to her trailer and got inside. She laid her backpack on the table and went into her bedroom, where she retrieved a much smaller backpack made from a black, stretchy nylon. It held travel shorts and a shirt, which worked out to no more than an eighth of an inch wide when tightly folded and packed—hardly visible against the fur of her spine once she transformed. PJ also grabbed a collar made of easily pliable black elastic. The collar had a purple gem amid a silver setting. The gem was actually a voice-activated camera she had programmed to recognize a certain system of throaty growls she could make as a feline. Her growling signals were no louder than the whispering wind on a dark night and meant she could capture whatever her amber eyes saw before her, as long as she held her chin up.

This was all she needed: a change of clothes and her camera. The shorts and shirt were practical necessities in case she failed to make it home before she morphed again come sunup. Summer was easy. Winter was much tougher. Having no fur once she transformed and only travel shorts and a T-shirt, she'd once almost frozen to death during the walk home after getting herself stuck in a shed two miles away on a freezing January night.

PJ had thought about putting other essentials, like a credit card, in her cat-pack, but one morning she lost the pack after it was snapped off by a tree branch and fell into a creek. After that, she carried nothing but expendable clothes—and used more caution around tree branches. That time, she had been stuck naked in the middle of a field at sunrise. Fortunately, she had found an old blanket in a nearby barn and made it home without undue attention. All she needed was to have the nickname Peeping Jane replaced with something worse about streaking in the early morning sun. And, how would her brother, Robert, react? If she were found naked in a field far from home, she'd never be able to convince him foul play wasn't at work and he need not investigate. That was one of the downsides of having FBI in the family.

PJ put the collar around her neck and the cat-pack on the floor. She sat near the door and watched the last light of day receding through the high branches surrounding her trailer.

At sunset exactly, she felt her shoulders give way, narrow and dip, and her pelvis lift. Her head flattened, and her ears raced backward and lengthened. Her snout elongated as all the while she was shrinking and shrinking out of her clothes, until the collar was no longer tight and the elastic held it gently against her furry neck. She squirmed into the cat-pack, nosed open her cat door, and stepped onto the small concrete stoop in front of her trailer. The air was muggy and hot; her fur seemed damp upon leaving her air conditioning behind.

She looked around. The sun had set, but the air was still alight with the grayness of dusk. As she reposed on her haunches, a woman walked by with a boy in tow. PJ recognized Maija Tate and her son, Alex. Although Alex was sixteen, he had the mind of a much younger child.

He pointed at PJ. "Mommy, look! A kitty." He rubbed thumb and fore-fingers together hopefully. "Kitty!"

His mom had a grip on his other arm and dragged him forward relent-lessly. "Alex, no. We're not stopping for a cat."

"Backpack. Backpack!"

PJ thought Alex was probably referring to the small black cat-pack she wore. She was impressed the boy could make it out in the dim light.

"No, Alex, we don't need your backpack," Maija said. "Mommy has hers. Now come on, otherwise we'll be late for the carousel."

The pair headed off toward the main gate, Alex shuffling along beside his determined mom.

PJ left her perch on her stoop and headed into the underbrush sur-rounding her lot. She was sniffing around when she heard the approach of a large animal. The animal wasn't trying to mask the sounds he made crashing through leaf and vine on his way toward PJ. PJ's whiskers stood to attention, and she sniffed the air in the direction of the commotion. Shortly, a Saint Bernard mix emerged from the trees and stood before PJ.

Hey, Mutt. What's new? she said.

Nothin.' What's new with you?

It wasn't that PJ could understand or speak animal languages per se, because they were so rudimentary compared to human language. Everything PJ thought in her head seemed to have a translation, but she'd noticed that the more complicated the thought, the simpler the resulting meows, and there were countless distinct ideas that seemed to have the exact same translation. She had no idea how her cat mind translated her very human thoughts into odd sequences of meows, yips, and growls. Chalk it up to the magic of her ability. She had spent some time writing and studying the translation process, trying to capture herself on tape and painstakingly making a dictionary. What she ended up with were the basics. As a person, she could reliably tell an animal five things: *don't groom here*, *food over there*, *enemy alert*, *sleep well*, and *I'm in heat, take me now*—the last of which she never used in practice, of course. She had no interest in producing litters of freaks like herself. She didn't figure she would be a great procreator and didn't even want to imagine how her shifts might affect pregnancy.

Mutt sat down in front of PJ. She noticed he still had his collar around his neck, and a length of cord ran down his side and away from him into the underbrush.

I see you broke out again, she said.

Uh-huh, uh-huh. Mutt's giant tongue lolled from his mouth, attempting to dispel some of the evening heat.

Mutt was a Saint Bernard mix that had wandered into Stoker Hills one January, half-starved and all attitude. Of course PJ couldn't leave him alone to the winter. She fed him and taught herself enough dog variations on animal language over the next few weeks to cajole him into becoming something like a pet. That was three years ago, and he'd mellowed to the point where he actually let her put a collar and leash on him. Looking at the broken end of the cord hanging from his collar, PJ realized she should probably use a metal chain instead.

She said, *You know, you're wearing a breakaway collar. You don't have to chew through the cord. If you just pull hard enough, you'll get out easily.*

I know. But the last time I did that, you were mad at me for ruining it.

Well, those things are expensive. But, never mind. Are you ready for our mission?

For the last few weeks, there had been random break-ins in Stoker Hills. PJ was angry, but even more curious. She thought she had an idea who it was. She figured it was Trent, the seventeen-year-old high school dropout three trailers down from her who hung out with some very unsavory characters. Trent was brother to Alex, who had recently passed with Maija on their way to the festival. PJ thought it significant that Trent wasn't with them. He's probably staying in the Hills to cause trouble, she thought. In this case, she wanted to catch him and his buddies in the act. She wanted to film them, get some unequivocal evidence of their thieving ways. What she would do with the evidence, she hadn't yet decided. She supposed there were at least three avenues to explore. Going to Maija was one option. But Trent and Alex's dad was MIA, and Maija was an overworked caregiver who looked after Alex full time. PJ didn't figure Maija would be able to corral Trent-the-irresponsible, since she already showed no sign of being inclined to do so.

It was too much, stealing from the neighborhood and terrorizing old Mrs. Cuthbert who lived in trailer 257 and nearly had a heart attack over their violations, not to mention over the loss of her wedding rings. Something had to be done, and PJ knew she was given her special power to address such things, FBI brother telling her to butt out notwithstanding.

Another option was to go to Trent himself and explain how he'd be tarred and feathered if he didn't desist immediately. Being an optimist, PJ favored this approach. Unfortunately, she'd already tried to broach the subject with him and had been told to screw off, but not in such nice terms. That left reporting him to the authorities or, in fact, going for the public tarring and feathering she had alluded to in her not-so-successful conversation with Trent. Being an optimist had made her approach Trent first; being vengeful would make her go with the last option. She planned to publicize her footage of Trent's thievery, once she obtained it. Decades of spending half her life as a cat had made her more than a little conniving, with a confidence far beyond that of a normal person. The sheriff, deputies, and FBI were her best friends and family, so she doubted she'd suffer any serious repercussions from Trent and his friends.

PJ was flooded with excitement at the prospect of catching the thieves in the act. She'd been patrolling the park at night for weeks, finding nothing, exasperated with herself when they broke into a trailer just next door to where she'd stopped for a catnap five days ago. Not tonight. Tonight she'd resist Morpheus and keep her amber eyes trained and her cat ears peeled. What were supernatural senses for a human were natural for a cat, and the thieves wouldn't get anywhere near her home turf tonight without her knowing. She was virtually certain that the festival would bring out the thieves, since they'd be expecting most trailers to be empty of fairgoers. If PJ were a thief, tonight would definitely be one of her target nights.

Mutt watched PJ as she cogitated. He panted and waited. Finally, when she seemed to be nearing the conclusion of her introspection, he spoke up.

What's the plan, PJ? Do you have one?

Of course I have a plan, you big galoot.

Mutt raised his chin and barked, two short, voluminous woofs.

Mutt, did you just thank the moon?

Maybe.

Weirdo.

Hey, don't knock it until you've tried it.

PJ briefly glanced overhead where the crescent moon was eclipsed by a dark cloud. She shook her head.

Anyway, she said, *Trent hates me, right?*

Hate is too strong. I think he would push your human face in some dog food, but not bite your genitals off.

Right. Anyway, they won't break into our trailer with you sitting out front.

But I'm not out front. I broke the cord and got away.

Exactly.

Huh?

PJ sniffed loudly. *You're not guarding our trailer. So I think they're going to consider it a prime target.*

Isn't that a bad thing?

Not in this case, because we're going to catch them in the act.

And bite them!

PJ flicked her ears. *No, we're going to film them.*

Oh. That's not as fun.

Come on, let's look around.

They started a slow circuit of the ten acres encompassing Stoker Hills. PJ wove in and out of trees, through yards, under cinderblocked trailers, and under decks and swing sets. The scene was indistinguishable from a cloudy day to her because the crescent moon was still bright enough that her cat eyes missed nothing. Mutt followed PJ as best he could, his powerful nose to the ground.

At the other end of the park from PJ's trailer was a dingy, rusty single-wide with a car on blocks and assorted metal junk in its front yard. It was owned by a cantankerous old gentleman by the name of Chip Greene. PJ always thought of "Greene" as in "green with envy" because the man seemed so sour by nature and constantly derided others for their possessions.

PJ was sniffing a twisted piece of metal that seemed to be a rusted truck bumper when there was a loud bang. Behind her, Mutt dropped to the ground with a shrill whine. PJ's mouth fell open. Had Mutt been shot?

Mutt! she yelled.

More shots followed. One zinged by and another pinged off the bumper PJ had been sniffing. Tears stung PJ's eyes.

Mutt! Mutt!

She ran over and started licking his prostrate form. More shots echoed through the night, all of them wide. Then, suddenly, Mutt jumped up and started running. PJ followed as closely as she could.

Two more shots chased them off Greene's property. Both volleys were swallowed somewhere in the night air, neither coming close to the animals.

When PJ and Mutt were halfway back to PJ's trailer, Mutt stopped to catch his breath. PJ came up beside him.

What happened? Are you shot? Are you bleeding?

Mutt sat back on his haunches and started licking his side furiously. *A bullet grazed me,* he said, *but it didn't break through my fur.*

PJ looked back in the direction of Greene's trailer. *Darn that old fart. He should be more careful. He could have killed us.*

It's just normal for him, though.

PJ nuzzled her friend. *I almost lost it. I thought you were killed.*

Mutt stopped licking his side for a moment to plant a giant, wet lick on PJ's head. She shook her head furiously after he retracted his tongue.

Ew.

* * *

At last they came back to PJ's trailer.

Okay, time to hide and wait, PJ said. *You sure you're okay, Mutt?*

"Woof!"

Shh, not so loud.

PJ climbed a large ash tree at the edge of her trailer's lot. Mutt pushed into the underbrush until all that could be seen of him was his black-peppered snout. They waited. PJ cleaned her ears and face thoroughly. After several minutes, she called down to Mutt.

Shh—stop it.

What?

You're panting. I can hear it from up here.

I'm hot.

Well, can't you pant more quietly?

"Woof!"

They'll hear you, dummy.

Mutt gave a soft whine and rested his face on his forepaws.

Less than an hour later, PJ was nodding off, and Mutt was antsy.

"Woof!"

PJ's eyes flew open. *What?!*

I smell someone. They are smoking.

PJ sniffed the air carefully. *I don't smell anything.*

That's because your nose is inferior.

PJ huffed. *Fine. Where are they?*

Mutt raised his face and spent a moment with his nose rapidly pulsating, like a frenetic accordion. *They're close. About five lots down.*

You can smell them from here?

All the way to the other end of the park.

Mutt got to his feet and shook himself. The jingle of his collar seemed very loud to PJ in the stillness of the Hills. *Shh,* she warned.

I can't stand this waiting. I'm going to check out that smoker.

Mutt, no.

But it was too late. Mutt had already broken from his hiding spot and was shuffling through the undergrowth toward whatever he smelled. It wasn't long before he disappeared behind a nearby trailer. PJ sighed and settled back down to wait. I hope Mutt doesn't scare them off, she thought.

* * *

PJ was half asleep by the time Trent and another youth showed up at her trailer. Their whispering gave them away. Her eyes snapped open, and she pushed forward on her branch, her whiskers vibrating meaningfully.

"Which one is it?"

Trent answered his friend in a low voice. "This one. I don't see that stupid dog anywhere."

"Okay, give me a second."

Trent's friend was significantly shorter than him. PJ could make out that he had darker hair and skin than Trent, but not much else. They were both wearing oversized T-shirts and Bermuda shorts with baggy pockets. Trent's sneakers glowed in the night dimness; the other boy's footwear was indistinct. It took him only a minute to pick the lock to PJ's trailer, deadbolt and all.

Jeepers, PJ thought. Is that how safe I am? And where was Mutt? PJ didn't smell any cigarettes and wondered if Mutt was off on a wild goose chase, following his nose to someone else.

Since she had first caught sight of Trent and his friend, she had been filming. She held her head in the air to give the camera in the gem of her collar a good view. She looked down her nose at the invaders. Once they'd picked the lock, they went inside quickly, shutting the door behind them. PJ wondered how long she'd be filming a closed door. She knew the infrared setting on her camera seemed to use more battery than the normal setting. She hoped the boys would come back out and incriminate themselves before the camera's tiny battery gave out.

Minutes passed. PJ stopped filming. After another interminable wait, she heard the door rattle and immediately turned her camera back on. The door opened, and Trent emerged, clearly holding one of the sleek cat figurines PJ collected.

"I like this one better," he was saying to the boy behind him.

The short boy emerged from the doorway just after Trent, holding out his hand. "Nah, this ring is way cooler." Ring? PJ squinted down her nose at the short boy. On the second-to-last finger of his right hand, she could make out a blocky ring.

Oh, no, she thought. Not Dad's class ring. Anything but that.

Her whiskers shuddered in protest. She moved forward, subconsciously ready to pounce and scratch the short boy's eyes out. She had to work to get herself to stay on her branch, steadily filming.

Suddenly, the sound of heavy paws on gravel filled the air.

"Woof! Woof! Woof!"

Mutt came running from behind PJ's trailer toward the boys.

"Oh, shit!" Trent screamed, all pretense of stealth forgotten as he raced down the steps and ran.

"Ahh!"

The short boy followed Trent, arms waving and pumping furiously as he sprinted to catch up.

Mutt chased them off the stoop and down the driveway, but then stood at the edge of PJ's lot and barked at them as they receded into the distance. PJ was sure the entire park would wake up at Mutt's vigorous yelling.

Mutt! Mutt! she cried, making her way down from her perch. *Stop!*

"Woof!"

He didn't stop barking until she came up beside him and gave him a bop on the nose.

Ow! he said in a sharp whine.

Quiet! Do you want the entire neighborhood to be here? You know my neighbors have already complained about you. Do you want animal control sniffing up our butts?

No. Mutt hung his head. *Did I do bad? Did you catch them on film like you wanted?*

PJ stared into the darkness in the direction the boys had escaped. She certainly hoped she got some good footage. She hoped it would be clear what the boys were doing.

We'll see, she said. *Tomorrow.*

3

Repercussions

Two days later, PJ sat in a booth at Coffee on Main, one of her favorite cafes on Main Street. It was newly renovated with big, plush booths and a pastel green interior. Above her, a big ceiling fan lazily circulated the warm air. She watched as her brother, Robert, came through the double glass doors from outside. It was another rainy day, and water drizzled from a gray sky. Robert shook off his umbrella and left it in a canister by the inner door. He looked around and discovered PJ sitting in a corner, then came over. He was carrying a newspaper. He smacked it down on the table in front of PJ and plopped himself into the booth across from her.

He was tall, six-one to PJ's five-one, and good looking, with a bony jaw and bright sienna eyes. Robert's dark hair was streaked with gray, and today he had it slicked back like a fifties greaser. PJ would have chuckled, but it was clear from his demeanor that today he would brook no sass. He sat heavily and motioned to the waitress for coffee.

"What in the heck did you think you were doing?" Robert asked.

PJ decided to play dumb. "About what?"

Robert pointed at the newspaper. It was yesterday's edition of the *Mayhap Mirror*, replete with photos of the Stoker Hills break-in video all over the front page.

PJ smiled. "Oh. That."

Robert sighed. "Damn it, PJ. What were you thinking?"

"I have no idea what you're talking about. The footage arrived in my inbox Sunday morning. I couldn't very well ignore it, so I wrote an article about it and submitted it to the *Mirror*."

The *Mirror*'s editor-in-chief published all of PJ's incredible photos. It was standing supposition that PJ took the pictures and video herself, but officially, PJ claimed an anonymous source mysteriously populated her email inbox with them. Of course PJ's journalistic integrity wouldn't let her reveal her source's address. So far, no law enforcement agency had tried to force her. She figured since she was obviously on the side of law and order that she was safe from prosecution. Or so she hoped.

Robert crimsoned. "You could have been killed. Where were you? Up in a tree or something?"

"I had nothing to do with the footage. I was as surprised as you were when it appeared."

Robert frowned. He stared at her, his light brown eyes fiery with indignation. His eyebrows rested heavily over his upper lashes.

PJ had gotten footage of the entire incursion. The front page of the *Mayhap Mirror* was filled with images of the break-in, from Trent and the short boy picking the lock on PJ's trailer to Mutt chasing them down the steps and off the property.

"Do you realize they can sue you for libel? They haven't been convicted of anything—or even arrested yet."

"I was careful not to state an opinion of what they were doing. I simply drew attention to the images, and the reader can judge for themselves."

The waitress dropped off coffee for Robert and refreshed PJ's. Robert nodded his thanks and immediately took a generous slug of the soothing liquid. After he swallowed, he said, "You're unbelievable."

"I would say the police have more than enough probable cause now."

"We should also have you arrested for aiding and abetting."

"What?!"

"Did you call the police from up there in your tree?"

"Uh. . . "

If paws could work a smartphone, PJ would have.

"See? Aiding and abetting. So you're basically an accomplice who turned sour after the deal went down. If they decide to gang up on you and blame you as the ringleader, you're totally screwed, sis."

"Is that your professional opinion?"

Robert was silent.

PJ looked down at her coffee. "I wasn't even there, Robert. I didn't take those pictures."

"I know that's your story. If you weren't there, where were you?"

"I was out looking for Mutt."

"See, here's the problem with that. You claim to have issues with darkness. And it's dark in the pictures, PJ."

"Well, I was wearing a headlamp. I can be out in the dark for a little bit, you know. I've been working on my phobia diligently. And I really wanted to make sure Mutt was okay."

PJ recalled the mean old Greene shooting at them with his gun and grazing Mutt. She shuddered. One day Greene might have better aim, and where would poor Mutt be then?

Robert interrupted her macabre reverie. "So you have no alibi."

PJ shook her head. "I won't need one. I'm sure Trent and whoever his friend was won't be clever enough to think of all this. By the way, do you have any idea who the second boy is?"

Robert ignored her question. "I'm clever enough to think of implicating you. And the boys' lawyer will no doubt be cleverer than I am."

PJ was annoyed. Robert might know who the short boy was, but due to professional responsibility to his organization, she was sure he wouldn't tell her unless he had a good reason.

"Come on, Robert, we both know no one's cleverer than you. That's why you got to pick your assignment and come back home."

"You're in serious danger here, PJ."

"They'd have to prove I took those pictures. I received them anonymously in my inbox, as usual."

"Sure. And if they search your computer, they won't find any traces of the files, right?"

"Heavens no." At least, thought PJ, not in any unencrypted format.

"And if we try to find out who sent those pictures, we'll hit a brick wall?"

"Right."

Robert flashed her a brief smile. "Good girl."

She laughed. "All that was just to scare me into being cautious?"

"Even if you're not arrested over this, you're never, ever going to live down the Peeping Jane title, are you?"

"Actually, I like PJ. It suits me."

Robert's eyebrows raced up his forehead. "It does?"

"It could also stand for 'photo journalist,' you know."

PJ gave him her brightest smile.

* * *

The next morning, someone banged on PJ's door at eight. She'd only gotten home a scant hour previously and awoke groggy and confused. The banging sounded again, and she nearly fell out of bed. From the commanding loudness of it, she figured it was Robert, probably come to chew her out again for the article on the theft. She stalked through her living room, put on her bathrobe, and threw open the door, hair wild and flying.

"You—"

She stopped short, already thoroughly regretting her appearance. It wasn't Robert. It was someone new. Someone in a police uniform. Someone with emerald eyes and tawny brown hair. Someone tanned, with full lips and a square jaw, whose physique could have been on the cover of a fitness magazine.

"Uh," PJ stammered.

She blushed. Very clever, she thought. I'm sure I've already won him over with my incredible vocabulary, not to mention my crazy hairdo.

The man smiled. The day was gray and spitting with rain, but with that smile, PJ felt like the sun was out and standing before her, radiating heat and light into her very heart. She practically started shaking.

"Hi," he said.

She was sure she must have the goofiest smile plastered on her face. It was nothing like the sun, rather probably like an obstreperous yard gnome. She was a yard gnome in the presence of the sun. She was amazed she didn't melt away completely into a puddle of stupid smile at his feet.

"Hi," she said.

"I'm Jake Tipton." Then, as if suddenly remembering who he really was, he added, "Detective Jake Tipton."

"You're on duty?"

What a stupid question. He was in a suit—of course he was on duty. PJ wanted to facepalm but found herself paralyzed, holding the doorjamb and bracing herself in the frame so she didn't fall down, thanks to her weak-kneed stance.

"Actually, I'm not due at work until nine, but I was up and ready and figured I'd stop by to see if you could answer some questions about the theft you had last weekend."

She glanced at the marked SUV behind him. In the back, looking out through the window, was a large German Shepard.

"Who's your friend?"

Jake shot a look over his shoulder. "That's Henry."

Comprehension dawned on PJ. "Oh! You're the K9, aren't you?"

Again, PJ had to suppress a nearly overwhelming urge to slap herself in the face. Empress Obvious strikes again, she thought. At this rate, she'd end up telling him that it was cloudy and a Wednesday. Way to waste the cute cop's time.

He smiled. PJ kind of wished she had a crime to confess so he would have to touch her to put on handcuffs and lead her to his SUV.

"That's me," he said. "The one and only."

At the festival, PJ had seen the K9 booth and the sign for demo times. She'd ignored it but now sorely regretted that decision. It would have meant many minutes of legitimately staring at Jake.

It was odd for a town Mayhap's size to have a K9 unit, but Jake was an animal lover and recent transfer, and had pressed for the privilege. PJ remembered the fundraising that took place last year and had even contributed to the new SUV and equipment Henry and Jake sported. She knew that the pair was already paying their way by sniffing out meth dens and even catching a man who had tried to flee into a horse barn on the west side of town. Henry had knocked the man down before he could do any harm to the horse he'd tried to take hostage. Imagine some idiot threatening to shoot a horse—for that alone, Henry was a hero in PJ's book.

PJ held her hands up to her ears and wagged them back and forth in what she hoped was a universal dog greeting. From the back of the truck, Henry barked once. She smiled.

"I think he likes you," Jake said. "That's darn unusual."

"Really?"

"Well, he's trained to be very suspicious. Normally, I can't let him out of the truck around people unless we're working."

"Let him out if you want. I've got treats."

At that moment, Mutt came wandering around the side of the trailer. He still had the chewed cord hanging from his collar. PJ took one look at him and knew he'd gorged himself on ravine water. His muzzle was twitching, and his eyes had a distinct greenish tinge.

"Oh, no," she said.

As Mutt neared, Jake said, "That's another reason to leave Henry in the car. He doesn't do too well with other dogs. He's definitely an alpha dog."

That sounded like most of the cops PJ knew as well.

"Mutt, no!"

Mutt retched. With a split-second warning, he barfed on the stoop, near Jake's feet. Dog vomit splashed on Jake's shiny shoes.

"Dang it!" PJ yelled.

Jake shook his foot, trying to get the splotch off. PJ grabbed Mutt by the scruff of his neck and growled at him. Mutt whined.

"Oh, don't be too hard on him," Jake said. "I should be used to it."

PJ dragged Mutt over to his doghouse.

"Get in there! Lie down."

Mutt hung his head, went into his doghouse, then turned around and lay down so his pleading mug was stuck outside staring up at them.

"Time to go inside," PJ said. "I'll see if I can find something to clean your shoes."

* * *

Outside, rain pelted the roof of PJ's trailer. Inside, she knelt before Jake with a wet washcloth and tried to clean his shoes.

"Oh, no," he said. "Don't do that. It's not your fault."

He took the washcloth from her and cleaned his shoes himself, then bused the washcloth over to the sink and rinsed it out thoroughly.

"Where's your laundry basket?"

PJ winced. Her bedroom floor was basically the laundry basket.

"Just leave it there. I'll get it later."

Jake sat again, at the edge of the dining booth. He pulled out a notepad and pen. He clicked the pen into writing mode.

"Some questions, please, PJ?"

"Uh, sure. But let me make us coffee first. I don't know about you, but I'm not really awake until I've had my first jolt of caffeine."

Jake smiled up at her. There went her knees again—the buckling seemed to be getting worse the longer she was in his presence, not better.

"Coffee would be great. Black, please."

PJ fired up the coffee maker and took her most expensive blend from the cupboard.

"Ask away. I'll try to answer coherently."

Jake chuckled. "Which night was the break-in again?"

"Saturday."

"Festival night. Of course. The news story ran when?"

"Monday."

"Oh yes, that's right." Jake watched PJ bustle around her small kitchen, preparing sugar and milk for her coffee. "Great story by the way. I laughed like crazy. The way you said people should draw their own conclusions. Hilarious. What conclusion could people draw but a burglary in progress?"

He laughed. PJ smiled.

"Anyway," he said, "what was taken? Anything of value?"

PJ blushed. He probably figured since she lived in a trailer, she had nothing of value to steal. But she did. She had a bevy of cat figurines and a collection of fine, shiny pieces of jewelry that fiercely appealed to her feline side. They were hidden all over her trailer. She thanked her lucky stars that the boys found only a tiny fraction of her treasures.

"A cat figurine and a class ring," PJ said. "But they dropped the figurine when Mutt chased them away, so just the class ring."

Jake scribbled in his notebook. "Was the figurine all right?"

"No, it smashed on the gravel where they dropped it."

"Oh. I'm sorry about that."

"It was one of my favorites. You can still see the pieces out there. I haven't had the heart to clean them up yet."

Jake nodded as he wrote a little more. "Where were you?"

The curt question caught PJ off guard. She almost forgot the alibi she had cooked up.

"Uh, I was outside, looking for Mutt."

"You were outside? When they were breaking in here?"

"Yes."

"About what time was that?" Jake's pen was poised above his notebook.

PJ swallowed. "I'm not really sure. I think it was just before midnight."

Jake's gaze dropped to his notebook as he wrote that down. "After eleven but before midnight. You can't be more specific than that?"

PJ shook her head. "No, sorry."

"And before that?"

PJ blinked several times at Jake. "What?"

"I mean, where were you before that? At the festival?"

"Oh, uh, no. I left the festival before sundown."

"But you were there?"

"Yes, with Vicky and Clara."

"I'm sorry. Vicky and Clara?"

"Vicky Donnerweise, surely you know her. She's a deputy."

"Oh, right. Of course. And Clara?"

"She's just my friend. Clara Goodwind. She's the assistant librarian."

"I don't think I've met her yet."

"How long have you been here?"

"Ten months."

"You must not go to the library much." PJ blushed. She wasn't supposed to be the one interrogating. The coffee gurgled and burped out of its filter. It was almost done.

Jake smiled at her. "Not yet, I admit."

PJ poured two mugs of coffee. Jake took his black, but she took a ton of cream and sugar. She always liked just a little bit of coffee flavoring with her cream and sugar. PJ sat across from Jake in the booth, and for a moment they watched each other drink. Jake took a fair sized swallow of coffee. PJ sipped hers delicately.

"Not bad," Jake said. "Smooth."

"It's Costa Rican," PJ said.

Jake nodded. "So you came home from the festival around sunset. When was that?"

PJ had the exact times of sunset memorized, but she didn't want to show it. "Around eight."

Jake put his coffee down and wrote in his notebook. "All right. Just one more question. Where were you between then and the break-in?"

PJ blinked several times. "I was here."

"I thought you said you went to look for Mutt?"

"Well, yes, but that wasn't until about eleven."

"So you were here in the trailer until then?"

"Yes."

"Why did you leave the festival so early?"

PJ was silent for several moments. She sipped her coffee and stared all around the room, purposely not looking into Jake's intent green eyes.

"Brooke?"

PJ started at Jake's use of her real name. "Wow. No one calls me Brooke. It's always PJ."

Jake wrote that down. "All right. PJ?"

PJ bit her lip. Next came the part where she had to explain how she couldn't ever be normal company after it started to get dark. And there went her chances of ever having a date with this cute cop, let alone getting married, having three kids, and living into ripe old age on the porch of a beautiful two-story house in north Mayhap. Not that I'm getting a little ahead of myself, PJ thought.

PJ cleared her throat. "I can't be in the dark."

"You can't be in the dark? What does that mean?"

"It means I need to be here, inside in the light, when the sun sets."

Jake stared at her for a moment. "You can't be in the dark?"

"I'm surprised you haven't talked to Vicky more about me."

"Oh. Well, I just know you and she are friends."

"I'm her odd-ball friend, that is."

Jake smiled. "You seem normal to me."

PJ wanted that to be a compliment. She smiled, saying nothing.

"Not that there's anything wrong with being afraid," he said.

"It's more than being afraid; it's a full-blown phobia. I have to stay here and sleep with my light blinders on."

"Light blinders?"

"They're like sleep masks people put on to sleep, but they make more light, not less. I always keep a pair around."

"Show me?"

"Sure."

PJ ducked into her bedroom and came back out with one of her self-made light blinders. Not that she ever actually used it at night, but she had to have a fully formed alibi for her nightly disappearances. It was a normal sleep mask like the type people bought for airplane trips, but she'd attached a string of battery-powered LED lights to the inside. She handed it to Jake. He turned it on and donned it.

"Wow. That's bright."

"It's some kind of physiological thing."

"You seeing someone about it?"

PJ blushed. "That's really personal."

"Oh, sorry." Jake took a swallow of his coffee. He watched PJ. She squirmed under his gaze, sipping her coffee self-consciously.

"I just have a little bit of a problem, but I'm sure you can clear it up," he said at last.

"A problem?" PJ said. Her voice seemed an octave higher than it should.

"Well, yes. I mean, you can't go out after dark, right?"

PJ stared at her coffee cup. "Yes."

"Yet you went out to look for Mutt at eleven, right?"

"Oh." PJ inhaled sharply. "I see what you mean. That sounds like a contradiction, doesn't it?"

Jake smiled. "I'm sure there's a simple explanation." He waited.

PJ swallowed. "Well, I've been experimenting with going out at night. Just a little bit. I've made myself light goggles."

"Light goggles?"

"Like the blinders, but they're goggles. Want me to show you?"

"No need, I can imagine." He wrote in his notebook. Upside down, PJ saw the phrase "light goggles" appear amid the flowery scribbling.

"Anyway, using them plus a flashlight, I can be outside for a little while before I get too freaked out."

"Okay. So you went to look for Mutt with your light goggles at eleven."

"I was worried about him. He goes into the ravine to drink, you know, and right now it is more of a raging river than a tiny creek."

"Okay." Jake was focused on his notebook. He said nothing else.

PJ waited, watching him write.

At last, he finished and looked up at her. He picked up his coffee mug and swigged from it. "Okay, I think that's everything."

PJ sipped her coffee. "I was only gone for a few minutes."

"Did you find him?"

"What?"

Jake ran his hand through his tawny hair. "Did you find Mutt?"

"Oh. Well, yes. When I came back to the trailer, I found him standing at the end of the driveway barking and barking. I guess he'd just chased the thieves off."

"And you found the cat figurine they dropped."

"Stepped right on the pieces. I recognized part of the head, my poor little cat."

"That's too bad, I'm sorry for your loss. When did you find out the class ring was missing?"

"I searched the trailer when I got back."

"You didn't call the police?"

A twinge of fear ran through PJ. This was really more of an oppositional questioning than she'd like. She remembered Robert's cautioning that the authorities could easily view her as an accomplice rather than a victim. She studied Jake carefully. His expression was open, his green eyes seemed on the friendly side of neutral. But he was a detective. Perhaps he was very good at seeming friendly right up until the moment he captured his prey.

PJ cleared her throat. "I was stressed out from going outside. From being in the dark. Frankly, when I found the ring missing from my jewelry case, I was too disappointed to do anything but lie down and sleep."

"Oh, your jewelry case. Can I see it?"

PJ bristled. Her bedroom was a veritable tornado of clothes and bedding. She didn't want Jake to see how messy it was.

"I can bring it out here if you'd like."

"Actually, I'd like to see the scene of the crime if you don't mind."

"I do mind." The words were out before PJ could censor herself.

Jake lowered his chin and gazed upward at her; the effect was to intensify his already intent gaze. "You do mind?"

PJ stood up. "You know, I'm getting a headache from all this questioning. Could you please leave? We can talk another time."

Jake stood. He looked at PJ for several moments, and she was suddenly afraid. She'd invited a cop into her house. What if he wouldn't leave? He was much bigger than her, probably at least six feet tall and muscular. She took a deep breath to calm her pounding heart.

Jake seemed to realize the effect he was having on her. He flipped his notebook closed and put it away. "All right. No problem." He turned sideways and brushed past PJ toward the door. "I'll just see myself out."

When he was outside, PJ watched him out the window, through the rain. He climbed into his SUV, talked on his radio for several minutes, then finally backed out of her driveway and drove away. It was only then she realized she'd been holding her breath. She let it out in a long stream, closed her door, and leaned against it. She was shaking. What did Jake think? What had been the result of his questioning? What if Robert was right and he was about to arrest her?

A knock on the door interrupted PJ's musings. She opened it, expecting Jake with more questions. Instead, Alex Tate stood on the porch. He was carrying a big tote bag with candy bar logos on it and PJ realized it must be fundraising time. Twice a year, he went around the neighborhood and sold candy for a local autism charity. He held a couple of bars out and shoved them toward PJ's face.

"You buy?" he asked.

"Hi Alex," PJ said. "Sure, I'll buy some. How much are they?"

"Two for five dollars," he said.

"I'll buy eight," PJ said.

"Twenty dollars!" Alex said.

PJ grabbed a twenty dollar bill from her purse, which was hanging on a hook next to the door. Alex never met her eyes, but he smiled at her feet. PJ watched him walk down her front steps and over the walkway, her hands full of candy. He was a nice boy. Too bad his brother was such a bad seed.

She sat at the table and finished her coffee, her mind filled with dread. Her cat sense seemed to be warning her of something big coming, something overwhelming and horrible. She dearly hoped she was overreacting to Jake's questioning, but what if she wasn't?

4

Ravine-ous River

It rained heavily for the rest of Wednesday as well as Thursday. Friday the rain seemed to let up, and at dusk the sky was streaked with purple and orange amid tall clouds that didn't seem as threatening as ones previously. PJ was restless. She wanted to get outside. At sunset precisely, her change occurred, and she became small, furry, and black with gray stripes. She shimmied into her cat-pack and checked to make sure her camera was primed and ready. She expected it to be a boring, ordinary night, but one never knew.

PJ emerged outdoors and saw Mutt, who was chained to a stake outside his doghouse.

Hey, Mutt. What's new? she asked him.

He was licking his haunches. He was in an awkward position due to having his chain wound around his doghouse until he could hardly move. *Nothin'. What's new with you?*

I see you're tied up like a hog on picking day.

"Woof!"

PJ sat delicately and proceeded to wash behind her ears. *Want help?"*

Mut wagged his tail energetically. *Uh-huh. Uh-huh.*

Come on, then. Follow me.

PJ led Mutt around and around the doghouse, unwinding the chain and giving him his relative freedom back. He raised his chin toward the sky and barked two short, gruff syllables.

PJ said, *There you go thanking the moon again. But it was me who freed you.*

I like the moon.

PJ looked up and stared at the sky. *Where is it? I can't even see it behind the clouds. And isn't it almost a new moon tonight?*

Mutt shook his head in an easterly direction. *Bit of brightness behind that cloud over there.*

PJ looked. *Oh, yeah. I see it now. Maybe. Well, anyway, I'm off adventuring. Call if you need me.*

Sure. Have fun.

* * *

An hour later, it was fully dark, and PJ had been sniffing around Stoker Hills. She was only about a hundred yards from her trailer when she heard something that sounded like a goat bleating. Her ears pricked up. She followed the sound north, along the ravine behind the trailer park. All the recent rain had turned the normally docile creek at the bottom of the ravine into a raging river. She had to strain to hear over the rushing water.

PJ slowed and went into stalking mode. She knew she was near Chip Greene's trailer at the other end of the park from hers. She remembered how Chip had shot pellets at Mutt and her the previous weekend, and she was wary. She crept amid the underbrush, not making a sound.

"Baaa!"

There it was again. PJ saw two dark figures standing by the ravine behind Chip's trailer. She recognized them immediately. One was Alex, the Tates' autistic boy. The other was mean old Chip Greene himself. Chip was saying something to Alex, and it seemed like Alex didn't like it since he was bleating like a goat at whatever Chip was suggesting.

PJ crept closer so she could hear what they were saying.

"...was you, wasn't it, boy? Don't give me that helpless act. I know you're just putting one over on all of us."

"Noo, noo."

"You're a liar and thief just like your mom and your brother. Come here to try to sell me some cock-and-bull story about fundraising for your found-aysh-ion. I know that's a crock of lies."

"Foun-da-tion. For au-autism."

PJ saw that Alex was holding a large tote bag covered with candy bar logos. She recalled that every springtime the boy came around the Hills to sell candy for the benefit of some foundation for autism that was helping him with school. But usually Alex was with his mom when he was selling the candy. And usually it was during the day. Perhaps Alex hadn't been able to find Chip earlier. Or, more likely, Chip was avoiding the boy, and now Alex had finally cornered him. It served him right.

"You buy?" Alex asked. PJ was sure it wasn't the first time he'd asked.

Chip pushed Alex backward with both arms. "No! Get away from me."

PJ's ears flattened along her head. Alex stumbled backward. Chip was standing right on the edge of the ravine, and the reaction of his shove had him sliding backward. His arms flailed, and he almost slid into the ravine. PJ found herself hoping he'd fall in. A dunk in the dark water would probably do the old crank well.

Alex saw Chip sliding and jumped forward to grab him. Chip resisted the boy's advance.

"Get off me, you faker."

Chip's poorly timed backward motion had him sliding farther into the ravine. PJ heard a splash as Chip's back leg slid all the way into the water.

"Damn you," Chip yelled.

"Help," Alex said. He reached once again for Chip.

This time Chip grabbed Alex's hoodie sleeve. PJ guessed the old man realized he was in danger of going butt-first into the cold water.

Crack!

PJ jumped. What was that? It had sounded like a shot!

Chip's head rolled back, and he started falling into the ravine. Alex grabbed at him. Then Alex lost his footing and slid forward. Chip fell into the cold water, pulling Alex with him.

No! PJ yelled.

She ran from her hiding spot toward the men. Chip had lost his grip on Alex and was floating limp in the water. Alex was splashing and flailing, trying to keep hold of Chip and simultaneously pull himself out.

PJ ran in circles along the edge of the water where they were.

Help! Mutt! Someone!

Alex lost his grip on Chip, and the old man floated away quickly, dropping over a dip in the terrain and heading south. Alex splashed and splashed, becoming tied up in his large tote bag. He was moving out toward the center of the water where it was deeper. It was clear he was having trouble reaching the bottom.

PJ jumped in circles screeching and yelling at the top of her lungs. She dipped a paw in the water but quickly pulled it out.

Meanwhile, Alex was losing his battle with the rushing water, and Chip was nowhere to be seen.

"Baaa! Help!" Alex's voice was shrill, and PJ wondered why no one heard him. Chip's trailer was at the far edge of the Hills, and perhaps no one was home in the closest trailer.

Help! Mutt! Help us!

PJ wondered about the fabled dog hearing. Where was Mutt? Would he hear her cries all the way at the other end of the trailer park?

Alex lost what was left of his footing and was swept southward with the water. PJ yowled as loudly as she could and ran along the side of the raging river. Alex seemed to pick up momentum as he went; he was right in the middle of the river. He slid down the dip and picked up even more speed. He was bleating like a goat the whole way, and PJ was screaming as she followed along the bank.

Mutt! For the love of life, Mutt! Hear me! Help!

Alex was flailing his arms and kicking his legs to no avail. He came to an eddy near a rock. It looked like a disturbingly large whirlpool. PJ couldn't believe their tiny creek had turned into this in the last few days of rain and spring runoff. She ran in circles as Alex tried to grab at the slimy rock at one side of the eddy.

PJ was torn. What should she do? Should she run and try to get help? What human would help her? She would never be able to make them understand. What about Mutt? He was muscular, but would he be strong enough to swim in the raging water and pull out a big boy like Alex? And what was happening to Chip Greene, who had seemed to faint with that shot-like noise?

Alex's wet arms clung to the rock. PJ ran in small, tight circles howling and howling. Above Alex, a branch extended over the water. Alex's arm reached out, and he gripped the branch. He grabbed it with his other arm as well and started pulling himself up, sliding along the rock.

Oh, thank God, thought PJ. He's going to make it.

Then the branch broke. It splintered in Alex's hands, plunging him once more into the raging whirlpool. Alex screamed. PJ screamed. Alex was sucked down into the water and disappeared.

No! No! Help!

PJ had no idea how far they'd come from Chip's trailer. Were they even in the Hills anymore? Darkness had fallen, and there didn't seem to be any moonlight to help her eyes recognize the dim shapes around her. PJ would have been crying if she could. Alex was going to die right in front of her, and there was absolutely nothing—

"Woof!"

A lumbering black shape closed in from the south, crashing through underbrush and trees. He came to PJ, and PJ saw he had no collar. He must have finally taken her advice and broken out of the dang thing.

Mutt! Mutt! Help Alex! He's in that whirlpool!

Before the stunned animals, Alex was spit out of the whirlpool and continued southward. The water became shallower, and Alex tried to get his footing. He was half-drowned and fell over quickly. Mutt jumped into the water without hesitation and swam toward the soggy figure. Alex bleated pitifully. Mutt closed the distance in record time and grabbed a mouthful of Alex's hoodie.

"Who? Help?"

Mutt released the hoodie long enough to bark loudly, then he gripped it again in his powerful jaws.

Alex seemed to recognize Mutt. "Doggie! Good boy! Doggie!"

Alex threw his arms around the big dog's neck. Mutt's powerful limbs fought the current, and he slowly made progress toward the shore.

There's someone else, Mutt! Chip is down the river too!

Go get him PJ, I got this one!

PJ saw that Mutt and Alex had made it to shallow water and Alex was struggling to get his footing. Mutt dragged him farther ashore, and the pair flopped down in the mud.

"Yowl!" PJ said and ran along the bank. She had no idea where Chip was or what she'd do if she found him. She thought, why couldn't I have been a doberman? Or a Saint Bernard like Mutt?

She ran, crashing along in the mud and the leaves. Finally, downhill, she saw Chip Greene. The old man had washed up on the opposite shore. He was deathly pale in contrast to the black mud around him.

Mr. Greene! Mr. Greene! PJ yelled. Then she stopped herself. He wouldn't have recognized her yowling anyway, and would probably have wanted to shoot her for it.

Chip wasn't moving. And between them, the waters raged. PJ dipped a paw into the dirty water.

Ugh, no way.

She hated water. Besides, if the current could sweep away grown men and give a strong Saint Bernard a problem, what could she do?

Mutt! Mutt! Come here, I found him! she yelled.

Curiosity and fear were coursing through PJ. Was Chip Greene dead? Had he been shot? Could she lick his face and revive him with her sandpaper tongue? She so desperately wanted to get across the water. She looked above her and saw that there was a way. Downstream, two branches nearly touched above the dark water. She ran over to the tree on her side and scaled it, then tiptoed across the first branch. It dipped with her weight.

Oh, nuts.

She almost fell. Spray had wet the branch, making the path slippery and even more dangerous. She inched her way to the tip and—

—slipped!

She clawed at the tip and managed to grasp it with a couple claws of one paw.

"Rawr!" she yelled, pain thundering through her arm.

Mutt! Help me!

Her arm stretched out until she was almost touching the water with her hindquarters. The roaring foam drowned out her cries, and the darkness seemed to laugh at her effort.

Noo—

—and she was down. Her claws took a chunk of the branch with her, and she slid into the black water and was immediately washed downstream.

Help!

She gurgled between meows and thrashed and thrashed, trying to fight the current or even just steer herself toward shore—but, she didn't know where the shore was. At least she was light enough that she mostly floated through the rushing darkness. Then tragedy: A rock loomed, a black amorphous shape she saw only briefly before crashing into it headlong. She was sucked under the surface. There was water in her mouth and ears—water everywhere. She couldn't fight anymore. Her arms and legs were made of thickening concrete. Her mind reeled slowly, and darkness overcame her.

5

Bedraggled

By dawn the raging river had calmed significantly, having spent its wrath. A golden mist filled the woods behind Stoker Hills, and the gathering sunlight cast long shadows on the trees, the rocks, the leaves, and the naked female body lying in the mud on the shore beside the emptying waters.

A short, chubby girl stood beside PJ and poked her with a stick.

"Ow!"

The girl jumped backward and dropped her stick. PJ raised her bedraggled head.

"That hurts."

"S-sorry."

PJ looked around. A thin white fog shrouded the houses around them.

"Where am I?"

The girl pointed into the fog. "That's my house up there."

"Okay."

"Were you attacked?" The girl's eyes were wide, bright blue in the morning light.

"No. No, I wasn't. I just, uh, fell."

"My mom says whenever a naked woman is found somewhere, it means some man attacked her."

PJ still lay flat on her stomach, unwilling to raise her head more than a few inches. The last thing she wanted to do was flash this child her muddy nakedness. The stretchy collar with the big purple gem was tight around her neck. At least it hadn't fallen off in the water. PJ didn't know where her cat-pack was; it wasn't on her back like it was supposed to be.

"In this case, no. I wasn't attacked. I just fell into the water. I didn't realize how dangerous it was. I'm glad you stayed away."

"I was in my room last night."

"Good for you."

"Mommy said I couldn't go anywhere near the ravine because of the dam that broke."

"A dam broke?"

"Yeah, upstream. It was just a small one. Otherwise maybe we all would have been washed away."

"Oh." PJ glanced behind her at the tame waters. A dam breaking on top of all the rain they'd had lately would certainly explain how their peaceful creek became a raging, person-eating river.

"Are you sure you weren't attacked? Maybe someone pushed you."

"No, I just slipped, sweetie. And now I have to get back home. Do you think your mom might have a robe or something I could borrow for a bit? I'll bring it right back."

"She does have a bathrobe. It's warm and pink and fuzzy."

"That would be great. Why are you out here so early anyway?"

"I couldn't sleep. I wanted to see the water. It's really high. But I'm not stupid. I waited until light and kept my distance."

"Good girl."

"Okay, I'll go get you the robe." The girl turned toward the dissipating fog, her motion tossing her long blond hair over her shoulders. "I'll be right back."

* * *

When PJ made it back to the Hills barefoot and in a too long bathrobe that dragged along the pine needles and leaves, she saw a county cruiser parked outside the Tate house. In fact, Vicky herself was behind the car, pacing. PJ trotted over.

"Vicky! What's happened?"

Vicky looked PJ up and down. "Just got up? That robe's a bit too big for you, isn't it? But I like your collar. That's a nice purple gem."

"Thanks." PJ blushed. She was sure she looked strange in her muddy collar and ill-fitting bathrobe. She just hoped Vicky didn't make too much of her appearance. "What happened, Vicky?"

Vicky sighed. She ran her long fingers through her ponytailed hair, then replaced her hat. "We're not entirely sure at the moment."

PJ saw Jake Tipton's SUV was squeezed into the driveway as well. Henry eyed the women from the back. PJ waved at the dog, and he put his ears back and forth in greeting.

"Is Jake here?" PJ asked.

Vicky eyed PJ curiously. "Detective Tipton's inside trying to make sense of what Alex Tate is saying. Or, rather, attempting to say. That boy is hard to understand. Do you understand him?"

"Well, sometimes when he's upset, he bleats like a goat. Then you have to calm him down before he can talk again. Is his mom with him?"

"She's MIA at the moment. I need to get back in there. Did you hear or see anything last night?"

A jolt of fear ran down PJ's spine. Of course she had seen something. But she knew she had to be careful what she said. For starters, she wasn't even supposed to be outside in the dark according to her "affliction." PJ swallowed. What could she say that was helpful but noncommittal?

"I heard a shot, I think."

"A shot? Really?"

"I think so. It was around midnight."

"Did you call the police?"

"Well, no."

"No? Why not? No one ever seems to call us. The whole neighborhood could be up in arms, and we'd be the last to know." Vicky chuckled and hooked her thumbs into her belt.

PJ smiled. "It might have just been a branch breaking. Or, you know, there's that old man down at the end of the park with his air pistol. He's always shooting at some poor animal or other. I thought it might be him."

"You mean Chip Greene?"

"Yeah, him."

Something seemed to spark a recognition in Vicky, and she was silent for a moment.

"Penny for your thoughts," PJ said.

"It's just that Alex keeps saying 'green', over and over. Do you think he means Mr. Greene?"

"Wow. I don't know. Maybe?"

"And you think Chip Greene might have shot at something in the night?"

"Maybe. He hates animals. He's always hassling the squirrels and dogs that come into the park. He's a mean old man."

"Okay, I'll go check it out after we finish with Alex. Why don't you go get dressed? Fire up some coffee. I'll come talk to you afterward."

* * *

When PJ got back to her trailer she found Mutt shivering in his doghouse, still damp from his nighttime swim. She whined at him and brought him inside. He whined back and sat near the heating vent and licked himself. She got her dog brush, set her hair dryer on low, and knelt next to him to help him groom.

"Oh, how I wish you spoke English," she said to him.

He looked at her with wide brown eyes, sympathy and frustration evident in their dark depths.

As a cat, PJ had animal languages in her mind. She didn't know how her understanding got there any more than she knew how her power happened in the first place. But she could passably speak with most sentient members of the animal kingdom, domesticated specimens especially. Cows and owls, in particular, seemed to have a lot to say. As a person, however, PJ retained scant memories of only the basics. She could warn an animal or praise them or generally communicate about as well as any sensitive human could, but she couldn't converse about what was in their minds or anything specific about what they saw or felt. That meant she would have to wait until nightfall to find out what happened with Mutt and Alex after she'd left.

In the meantime, she groomed and fed Mutt. He slept on his back on his cozy dog bed in the corner, ears twitching, legs in the air.

After Mutt was taken care of, PJ headed to her bedroom, which also functioned as her study and workshop. She carefully removed her collar and popped the gem from its setting. Inside was her camera. Water had penetrated the setting and dribbled from it as PJ extracted the camera. She held it up to the light. It looked all right, but she knew it had been for quite a ride. She wanted to let it dry out thoroughly before she tried to extract any information from it. She opened up the camera and placed the pieces delicately onto a paper towel. She didn't know how long she should wait, perhaps a day or two. She was itching to see what the camera had captured, but she didn't want to plug it in prematurely and cause even more damage.

PJ was dressed and the coffee had fully percolated by the time Vicky knocked on her screen door. The main door was open, and PJ saw Jake's SUV drive away behind Vicky.

"Come on in, Vicky. Coffee's hot and ready."

Vicky removed her hat when she came in and placed it on PJ's dining booth. She helped herself to a mug and some coffee, then sat opposite PJ in the booth and sipped her coffee, black.

"Thanks, PJ. You're a lifesaver. You can never have too much caffeine in the morning, especially on a morning like this."

"So what happened? Did you get ahold of Chip Greene?"

Vicky pulled at her ear. "No one answered at his trailer."

PJ frowned. Had Chip survived his travel through the water like she had? Or was he somewhere downstream needing help? PJ had a decision to make. Either she had to pretend to know nothing more than what she could detect from her trailer, or she had to tell Vicky that she saw Chip fall into the water. She didn't think she could keep her mouth shut for several reasons. First of all, how could she leave a man lying in danger? She had to say something. Also, she was by nature a forthcoming person. She hated lying, even though she had to do it constantly because of her odd transformation. Finally, she thought the truth would have to come out eventually. Once Alex calmed down he'd speak of Chip falling in the water. PJ had already gotten herself involved by claiming to have heard the shot. She might as well own up now, to her friend, and tell what she could of the whole story.

"Vicky, I have to tell you something."

At PJ's serious tone, Vicky raised her face from the coffee cup. Vicky's bright blue eyes watched PJ carefully. "All right"

"I went to investigate when I heard the shot."

"I thought you were afraid of the dark."

PJ shook her head. She hated having to explain this part. She knew it was a hole in all of her stories a mile wide. "I am afraid. But I've been trying to get better. I took light goggles and a bright flashlight."

"Light goggles?"

"They're like ordinary plastic goggles, but I've put LEDs around them. I think it tricks my mind into thinking it's light out. Anyway, I can't be out that long, and it is very scary for me. But I'm working on trying to overcome my phobia little by little."

"Well, land's sake, PJ. That's good. So you investigated when you heard the shot. What did you see?"

"Not much. Having all that light right on my face means I can hardly see anything."

Vicky laughed. "I can imagine you with Christmas tree lights all over your face. Bet you'd give anyone who saw you a heart attack."

"Which is another reason I try to avoid everyone."

"Okay. So you went outside. Where'd you go? What'd you see?"

"I walked toward Chip's trailer. I saw Chip and Alex by the ravine."

Vicky's brow lowered, making her look very intent. "You saw Chip and Alex? Together?"

"I think so. It was in the distance. But, Vicky, here's the part I need to tell you. I think Chip fell in the water."

"What?!" Vicky put both hands on the table and leaned forward.

"I didn't see that well because of the goggles and the distance, but I really think I saw Chip fall in the water."

"What about Alex?"

"I don't know. They were just two muddled shapes at the edge of the ravine. Honestly, at the time, I almost thought they were just trees or bushes, but they moved."

"What did you do?"

"I was frustrated with myself because I couldn't see properly. I tried to take the light goggles off, but then I had a panic attack and had to come back here. I didn't see anything else."

Vicky rubbed her chin. "You really saw Chip Greene fall into the river last night?"

"I saw a figure that might have been a skinny man fall over and disappear. Then I couldn't see anything."

Vicky stood up. "We need to find Chip Greene. If you're right, we might need to start by dredging the water. This is big, PJ. I wish you'd come to me sooner."

"I'm sorry, Vicky. I wasn't sure what I'd seen. But when you said Alex was saying 'green', I remembered what I thought I saw."

Vicky was already on her radio calling for backup. After talking to the dispatcher, she said to PJ, "I hope you're wrong, PJ. I hope you're wrong."

6

What Mutt Smelled

When evening came, PJ transformed as always. She felt naked without her cat-pack and camera collar. She nosed her way through her cat door. Mutt was nowhere to be seen. She yowled in frustration.

Dang it, where is that canine?

She sniffed the air, but she knew she didn't have half the sensitivity of Mutt's nose. He could be nearby, and she wouldn't know it. She decided to set off in the direction of Chip Greene's trailer. When she got there, the area seemed deserted. In back, behind the trailer near the ravine, an area of mud was cordoned off by police tape. No humans were in evidence, but PJ found Mutt sniffing around in the cordoned-off section.

Mutt! You are wrecking their crime scene with your pawprints.

Mutt raised his head to look at her. *Huh?*

Oh, never mind. Do you smell anything?

Mutt returned to sniffing the ground. PJ stepped lightly past the tape and started sniffing around. She saw that the area they'd cordoned off included a lot of footprints.

I just smell humans. Alex and Chip stood here.

Well, we already know that, you big galoot.

"Woof!"

For a while, both animals were silent while they sniffed and sniffed. PJ got a feel for the layout of the area. The footprints did seem to tell the story. Alex's footprints were big sneakers with wavy treads. Chip's were flat-footed indentations of worn-out loafers. Both sets of footprints came into the area from the direction of Chip's trailer. There were deep footprints, a lot of them, in the space where Chip and Alex had stood talking. Then there were one or two very deep loafer prints; PJ was thinking those were from when Chip stepped into the water by accident and fell. The water had receded greatly so it was difficult to tell where the waterline had been when the very deep prints were made. Alex had also made very deep prints in the soft mud, more of them as he shuffled and struggled with Chip. PJ wondered how much of the story the police had garnered from these telltale footprints.

After sniffing to her heart's content, she stopped to rest at the edge of the area. Mutt was still energetically sniffing around. He seemed to be mostly sniffing his own paw prints. PJ saw that the ones he'd made the previous night were deeper than any he was making now. The story continued in Mutt's paw prints, which entered the area to the south in broad strides and raced right into the deep, dark mud at what used to be the water's edge. PJ recalled how Mutt had brought Alex out of the water. Mutt was a hero in her estimation.

Good job last night, Mutt.

Huh?

With saving Alex. I think he might have drowned if you hadn't pulled him out.

Oh, that. Thanks.

What happened after I left to find Chip?

Nothing much. Alex walked from the water toward his trailer. I followed you but couldn't find you in the dark. I smelled you for a while, but then your scent disappeared.

That must have been when she fell into the water, PJ thought. They walked south along the now sedate creek and found signs of Alex's egress from the water, along with Mutt's prints. These new prints weren't in a taped-off area, and PJ wondered if the humans had found them properly. They told the story of Mutt saving Alex. PJ's chest puffed out with pride in her friend.

Did you find Chip? she asked Mutt.

Nope.

But he was there. I saw him before I fell in the water.

Show me.

PJ led Mutt downstream to the slight bend where she'd seen Chip lying on the opposite bank of the water. She looked up at the branches nearly touching above the stream and nodded at them.

Those branches are where I fell from.

Mutt shook his head. His whole body followed. *I'm really glad you weren't hurt.*

Me too.

PJ noticed the absence of police tape around the scene across the creek. The water was shallow enough that a line of rocks spread across to the other side.

Let's try to cross.

Be careful, PJ.

PJ gingerly stepped onto the first rock. Water rushed past. She got her front feet wet jumping onto the second rock and howled in complaint.

Careful, Mutt said. He was simply fording the stream, getting the bottom half of himself wet and dirty.

PJ cautiously leapt to the last stone, then to the mud on the other side of the water.

Ugh. Now I have mud on my paws, she said, flicking first one front paw, then the other, in a vain effort to get the icky material off.

It happens.

PJ noticed that in spite of Mutt having been bathed that day, he was shaggy and dirty again. She sighed. Then she turned her attention to sniffing the imprints around the area.

This is where I saw Chip lying. I wonder if the others found him?

PJ expected to see the faint outline of a prone human in the mud. Instead, there were great streaks and whorls.

That's weird.

What?

He was lying right here, but there's no sign of it.

Mutt sniffed the area PJ indicated carefully. *I do smell Chip here, but it is very faint. Perhaps the water washed it away?*

But the water didn't come up here. I'm sure of it.

Mutt was still sniffing avidly. *Usually when scents are this faint, there's been water. It washes everything away.*

Hm. I suppose you could be right. And there are no footprints.

Yes, there are.

What?

Come. Mutt led PJ into the underbrush. Amid leaves and pine needles were a couple of small human footprints. They had flat bottoms and pointy toes. There were only two that PJ could find.

Who made these? They're too small to be Chip's, PJ said.

Mutt vigorously sniffed the two offerings. *I can't tell. They're human.*

Thanks a lot, Mutt. I could figure that out on my own.

Suddenly Mutt's head perked up. He sniffed the air. *There it is again.*

What? PJ smelled nothing other than the damp fecundity of the surrounding forest and the musty scent of drying mud.

Cigarette smoke.

Where?

Follow me.

Mutt led PJ back across the stream. He waited on the other side while she carefully navigated the rocks. Then the two of them scampered up the side of the ravine toward the trailer park and came up near the Tate trailer.

There, Mutt said, indicating the trailer.

Someone's smoking in the Tate trailer?

Outside, I think. Let's be quiet.

The animals snuck around the trailer and peeked into the front yard. Maija Tate had fenced off a small area of grass around her front stoop, and there were yellow flowers in a bed near the white picket fence. Outside the fence, leaning against Maija's brown hatchback, was the short boy from the robbery, smoking a cigarette. Trent was with him, also smoking.

Yup, Mutt said. *That's what I smelled.*

Cigarette smoke is yucky, PJ said.

Uh-huh. Do you know who that short boy is?

No. My brother probably knows, but he wouldn't tell me. He ignored me when I asked.

Your brother should question him about last night.

What? Why?

Because I smelled the same cigarette smell.

You did? When?

Before I jumped in the water to save Alex, on my way down. I passed an area that smelled like leftover smoke.

So somebody smoking had been nearby?

Not just somebody—that short boy.

How do you know? A lot of humans smoke.

Yes, but that short boy smokes cigarettes that smell different. Like right now. There is a difference between what Trent is smoking and what the short boy is smoking. Can't you tell?

PJ sniffed the night air carefully. *I can't tell anything but smoke.*

Mutt chuffed. Both boys looked over to where the animals were watching. PJ and Mutt quickly retracted their heads before being seen.

Shh, PJ said.

They had been talking with their ears, noses, and paws instead of their mouths, so they had made very little noise until Mutt's ill-timed chuffing.

Oops, Mutt said.

The animals retreated to the area behind the Tate trailer. The boys didn't follow or show any sign of investigating the noise they'd heard.

Why aren't they in jail, anyway? PJ said.

You published the footage of the break-in, didn't you?

Yes. But nobody seems to have done anything about it.

Mutt shook his head. *Humans.*

7

Oh, Brother

The next morning PJ visited the laundromat to wash the bathrobe she'd borrowed. Hardly anyone was there in the early hours of this Sunday morning. She put the robe in the washer and decided to check out what the newspapers were saying across the street at the gas station.

There it was, front and center in the *Alameda Sentinel*. PJ was very annoyed that her rivals had gotten the news before the *Mayhap Mirror*. Alameda was rival to Mayhap in more than one way, mostly through high school sports rivalries and proximity. The Indiana town pronounced its name Alameda to rhyme with Andromeda to distinguish it from that town way out West. PJ was immediately embarrassed she hadn't broken the scoop for the *Mirror* before the *Sentinel* got ahold of it.

The article had a picture of the concrete bridge over Mayhap Creek. Around the base of the bridge was a team of crime scene investigators working behind crime scene tape. PJ could make out a couple of people she recognized, as well as Jake Tipton, who seemed to be supervising. The man beside Jake was very familiar; it was her brother, Robert. He had his hands on his hips, and beneath his blazer, his badge and gun stood out. PJ wondered why the FBI was interested in the scene.

She thought she knew before she even read the article what might have happened. The text confirmed it. Chip Greene had washed up there, dead, at the foot of the bridge, and had been found the previous morning by an early jogger on the trails near the bridge. PJ's scalp tingled as she read, an effect she knew would have been confined to her whiskers if she were a cat. It signaled some kind of prescience about the future which she could never put into words.

Why was Chip found so far south? He had washed up where PJ fell into the river, a good half mile north. PJ tried to remember the exact scene. Could the water have dragged Chip back in? PJ didn't think so. He seemed very stable there, far enough from the rushing water not to be in danger. The larger question was, why had he died? PJ thought back very carefully. She was almost certain she remembered Chip's chest rising and falling in the dim night. Her cat eyes were perceptive enough to see that. She didn't think she had imagined it. So Chip was alive and upstream when PJ started her ignominious trip down the river. And, in spite of hitting her head and knocking herself out, she had washed up not far from where she originally went in, by the girl's house in the fog. How far had it been? PJ decided, when she dropped the bathrobe off, she'd better investigate back there.

* * *

It was almost two hours before the robe was washed and dried and PJ headed out to the blond girl's house. She didn't have a great excuse for having the robe and simply hoped no one would ask too many questions.

Their house was a typical American two-story in gray siding and white trim. The porch was large and surrounded with a white balustrade. PJ climbed the steps and rang the doorbell. She saw the front curtain move as someone quickly peeked out, then a dark figure showed through the frosted glass of the front door. The door opened.

It was the same girl who had found PJ.

"Oh, hello again," said PJ.

"Hi. My mom's in the shower. Want me to get her?"

Silently, PJ thanked her lucky stars. "No, I'm just here to drop off her robe. You can thank her for me, okay?"

PJ handed the bundle of pink fluff to the girl.

"Okay," the girl said. "What's your name?"

"PJ. What's your name?"

The girl's smile lit up her face. "Bridget. But everyone calls me Birdie. Isn't that weird? How do they get Birdie from Bridget?"

PJ chuckled. "Well, they're both very nice. But I have to go now. Make sure to thank your mom, okay?"

"Sure. I will."

"Bye."

The girl seemed reluctant to close the door. PJ waved again and turned to walk down the steps and sidewalk. Finally, she heard the door close, and when she glanced back, she didn't see anyone watching her through the windows.

PJ walked out to the main sidewalk, then to the garage side of the house which seemed sequestered from the front windows. She took a deep breath, then stepped into the lawn and went quickly past the house. There was no fence delineating the backyard, but they had a large playset. PJ moved through the space until she met the woods that lined the ravine, then stepped carefully into them. Poison ivy was everywhere in Indiana, and PJ knew she had to be careful not to get a foot full. She passed through a tangle of trees and brush and emerged at the top of the ravine. Carefully, she made her way down to where she thought she had washed up. She looked behind her. She could see Bridget's house up the hill, about a hundred yards away. No one seemed to be on the back porch, and as far as PJ could tell, no one was looking out any of the back windows.

PJ studied the area around the water carefully. She saw a deep indentation that could have been made by her body. She saw her own naked footprints as well as smaller ones in slippers that were no doubt Bridget's. Her cat-pack was nowhere to be found.

She walked north along the water's edge. She had to pick her way through mud and underbrush carefully. Some areas, the ravine was almost a vertical drop-off; at others it sloped more gently down from the line of houses to the east. PJ was sweating by the time she came to the place with the overhanging branches where she'd seen Chip and then fallen in. Counting her steps, she figured she was almost half a mile from Bridget's house. She had been in the water for quite a while in that case. She was lucky she hadn't drowned. Chip, apparently, hadn't been so lucky.

She looked southward. The ravine ran through a bend after this point, and she couldn't see very far down the waters. They looked treacherous, though, even though they'd died down significantly since PJ's trip through them. PJ looked up the sides of the ravine. Both to the east and west, the backs of houses were evident. Looking west, she wondered whose house backed up to where Chip had been laying.

As she stood and wondered, she suddenly felt a brush of fur against her leg. She jumped backward, startling a small black animal.

"Oh, goodness," PJ said. "Hello there, little kitty. You startled me."

The cat looked familiar. It was jet-black and looked like it couldn't have been more than a few months old. One of his eyes was sticky, and he blinked it often.

"I know you. You're the kitten I saw on my way back from the festival." PJ knelt and offered her hand. The kitten sniffed her fingers warily. PJ wished she could change into a cat at will so she could communicate better with this kitten. As it was, she made a trill sound and closed her eyes tightly, then opened them. She hoped she wasn't being too forward. The trill sound was a playful one, and she knew that when a cat wants to smile, it will close its eyes in front of you to show you it trusts you.

The kitten simply stared at her, not closing his eyes in return, but not running away.

PJ reached for the kitten. "We really should do something about that eye. It looks like the beginning of an infection."

At PJ's reaching hands, the kitten took off, jumping into the underbrush and stopping a few feet away. PJ knew she wouldn't be able to catch the cat if it didn't want to be caught.

"Well, maybe we'll meet again some night. Do you hang around by these houses? Do you belong to one of them?"

The cat said nothing, only staring at PJ with bright yellow eyes.

* * *

When PJ got back to Stoker Hills, a nondescript navy sedan was parked outside of her trailer. She squeezed her maroon GT next to it and got out. The sedan really screamed government. That could only mean one thing.

Before she could ascend her stoop, the door opened and her brother, Robert, accosted her.

"Where in the hell have you been?"

"Well, hi to you too, Robert."

He frowned. He stepped back so she could pass inside. He closed the door, and they looked at each other on the small patch of linoleum that PJ considered her foyer.

He said, "I've been waiting here almost an hour."

PJ held up her purse. "Did you try the phone?"

"A dozen times. You're not answering it. I saw why once I got inside."

"What?" PJ started rummaging through her purse.

Robert retrieved her smartphone from his jacket pocket and handed it to her. "It was in your bedroom, on your dresser. I heard it ringing."

"You went into my bedroom? You rifled through my things?"

"PJ, it was in plain sight. I didn't snoop any more than that."

PJ sighed. "So I forgot my phone at home. Did you find anything else interesting, in plain sight?"

"Well, I saw your camera."

"Oh. Crap." PJ recalled that she had taken it apart and left it on her desk to dry.

"Never mind that. Did you get any footage of what happened here the other night?"

"Footage of what?"

"Don't play dumb. I don't have the patience for it right now."

"You mean what happened to Chip Greene?"

"Of course that's what I mean."

"Sit down, Robert."

They eyed each other. Robert moved away from PJ and sat at the far side of her dining booth. She went to the counter. "I'll tell you, but let me catch my breath and make some coffee first."

"Fine." He stared out the big window over the dining booth.

A few minutes later, PJ had the coffee machine ready and working, and she sat down opposite Robert.

"You're not at church this morning?" PJ asked.

"Didi and Nanci went. I came here to get your side of the story."

Didi was Robert's wife, and Nanci was their twelve-year-old girl, PJ's niece. PJ loved Nanci. The girl had amber eyes like her, a great sense of humor, and the suppleness of a cat in both mind and body.

"What makes you think I even have a side of the story? Maybe I was at home sleeping?"

"PJ, whenever anything happens in this town, you miraculously happen to be there. Plus, I talked to Vicky. I know you saw the altercation."

"Altercation?"

"Between Alex Tate and Chip Greene."

"Like I said to Vicky, I didn't see it that well. I had my light goggles on."

"Light goggles?"

PJ got up and went into her bedroom. She came back with ordinary work goggles strung with LEDs. She put them on and turned the lights up.

"See?"

"You look like something that should go on top of a Christmas tree."

"So I've been told."

"What's the point of those?"

"Well, it's possible my darkness phobia is physiological. If so, having bright light always by my ocular nerve should lessen it."

"Is Doc Fred giving you this baloney?"

PJ turned off the lights and removed the goggles. "I don't want to talk about it if you're going to call it baloney. It might be working. I might be able to be outside in the dark."

"Looking like a circus freak, though."

"It's not perfect, I admit."

"PJ, it's perfectly weird. It's you."

"Gee, thanks."

The coffee pot gurgled, signifying the presence of coffee. PJ got two mugs down from the cupboard and filled them. She knew Robert liked his with a touch of sugar.

"Thanks," he said when she handed him his mug.

PJ topped her coffee with cream and sugar and sat down opposite Robert again.

"All right," he said, "I want to hear everything about that night."

"We're talking Friday, two nights ago, right?"

"You know we are."

"Don't get ornery. I'm trying to orient myself."

"Sorry." He took a sip of coffee.

"Well, I was out with my light goggles, practicing being in the dark."

"You were randomly out walking around?"

"Basically."

"Was anyone with you?"

"Who would be with me?"

"I mean, like Mutt."

"Oh. Yes, he was with me. He helps with the fear, as you can imagine."

"Yeah. So then what happened?"

"Well, we were walking north, toward Chip Greene's part of the park."

"Any particular reason?"

"Nope. Just walking behind the trailers in that direction, along the top of the ravine through the woods."

"Okay. So what'd you see?"

"I'm getting to that. When we came to Chip's trailer, I thought I saw Alex and Chip down by the water. But I was far away and couldn't really recognize them. I only realized who it was the next morning when Vicky was at Alex Tate's and said he was saying 'green' over and over. Then I figured who I'd seen were Alex and Chip."

"All right. Then what?"

"Well, nothing really. The one I now think was Chip fell in the water, and the other one—Alex—tried to help him."

"You saw Chip Greene fall in the water? Did you hear anything?"

"He was yelling at Alex to get away from him."

"Did you hear anything else?"

"Like what?"

"PJ, another neighbor heard a shot around that time. This would have been about midnight."

"Oh, how could I forget. Of course I heard what sounded like a shot."

"Sounded like a shot? You're not sure it was a shot?"

"It could have been a tree branch cracking. Or a hammer hitting something. You know, it was a loud bang. I can't say for certain it was a shot."

"We found Greene's handgun in the water."

"He shot at Alex?" PJ was surprised. She hadn't seen anything like that. But did she just miss the small gun in Chip's hand?

"Is that what you saw?"

"No. I was too far away, and with the light goggles, I can hardly see anything straight. I didn't see any weapon in Chip's hand that I know of. I know he almost always carries his gun with him, though, so if he fell in the water I'm sure it wouldn't have been far."

"Hm. How about in Alex's hands? Did you see the gun?"

"What!? That's ridiculous. Alex wouldn't hurt a fly."

"Chip Greene washed up at the bridge near Mayhap Road, dead."

"I know. I saw the *Alameda Sentinel* this morning."

"Why would he just fall into the ravine? There's talk he wouldn't—that he was either pushed or shot."

"Oh, for heaven's sake, that's crazy. What does Alex have to say about it? You need to ask him—he was there."

"You know how hard he is to talk to."

"He's autistic, but you can talk to him if you're patient. Why don't you get one of your shrinks to talk to him?"

"We might if we get him away from his lawyer."

"He has a lawyer?"

"You know him, too."

"I do?"

"Liam Pfefferheim."

"Oh." Liam Pfefferheim was legal counsel to anyone disadvantaged or down-and-out in the Indianapolis area, which included the residents of Stoker Hills. PJ had gone to grade school with Liam. Then she re-met him years ago when she interviewed him for an article about a Hills girl who'd been assaulted by someone from the mayor's office. The case had been hushed up, and Liam had seen to it that the entire nation had heard about it by the time he was finished, making him the eternal friend of Stoker Hills denizens and the eternal enemy of the Mayhap elite.

"Yeah. There's talk he might represent Trent on the theft cases, too."

"Oh, the thefts. I forgot all about those."

"We haven't. It's just taken a while to get the subpoena to go through the Tate trailer."

"And did you guys go through it yet?"

"Tomorrow."

"I hope you find Dad's ring. I want it back."

"I'll make sure they're looking for it."

"Why does Alex need a lawyer?"

"As I said, there's talk he pushed Greene or shot at him."

"That's ridiculous."

"You were an eyewitness, PJ. You could clear up a lot by coming forward and making an official statement."

"But I hardly saw anything."

"How about your camera?"

PJ cleared her throat. "I didn't have a camera."

"Sure you didn't. PJ, we all know you take those pictures. Stop with the bullshit about some anonymous photographer sending them to you."

"Fine. Maybe I do take a picture or two now and again. But my camera is waterlogged. I want to let it dry thoroughly before I even try to see what's on it."

Robert swigged from his coffee. He put the cup down and swallowed heavily. "In this case, I guess we're all waiting on pins and needles to see what your pictures will say."

"I know."

"And, in the meantime, can you at least talk to your friend Pfefferheim and get Alex to open up a little more? The silence is damning."

PJ sighed. "I'll try."

8

Pro Bono

Liam Pfefferheim's law office was at 38th and Lafayette in Indianapolis, wedged between an erotic pastries shop and a check-cashing place in an otherwise nondescript strip mall. It wasn't the greatest of neighborhoods. Sometimes the nearby Walmart parking lot was filled with panhandlers who spilled over into the mall. On those days, Liam offered them coffee and cookies until he ran out. He was doing well enough to have two assistants: a secretary who ran the front desk and a paralegal who helped him with everything else.

Liam's secretary, Jazmin Berra, was an imposing woman with thick, long black hair, watchful brown eyes, and an accent on the British side of Indian. She favored saris and eyeshadow in a dark spectrum—indigo or olive—and she complemented them with thick black eyeliner. Horn-rimmed glasses hung from a gold chain around her neck, and she was perpetually donning them and staring at whomever stood opposite her over their black-and-gemmed frames. When PJ walked in, there were no indigents, and Jazmin recognized her immediately. Her glasses were on, and she eyed PJ over their sparkly edges.

"Well, hello there, PJ. You're here to see him, I assume? Did you think to make an appointment?"

PJ laughed. "Not this time."

"You never make the appointment. Honestly, he is busy at the moment with a client; you will have to wait."

"Okay."

Jazmin actually seemed a little glad for the interruption. PJ wondered what she was working on.

"So," Jazmin said, "how is life south of Nowhere?"

Nowhere, Indiana, was a tiny hamlet five minutes north of Mayhap and rendered PJ's hometown the constant butt of boondocks jokes.

"Same as usual. But we had a bad accident a couple of days ago."

"The drowning in the creek?"

"Oh, you heard about that all the way down here?"

"I read an article; you know Liam still gets the *Mayhap Mirror* delivered here; there it is on our coffee table." She motioned toward the waiting area. "I am surprised your byline was not on it."

Among stacks of magazines PJ saw the larger folded newsprint of the paper. "Yes, well, I guess Sam beat me out this time." Aspiring feature writer Samantha Collins perpetually wore a red fedora with a white feather and was PJ's main rival for space in the *Mirror*'s pages. Sam tended to be more interested in art and interior design than crime, but if called upon, would swear an interest in anything from teapots to turkeys.

"I guess she did. And we all know about it down here. You can take the man out of the town, but the town stays with the man, right? Or at least the newspaper does."

PJ chuckled. "Well, Mayhap grows on you. What's new with you guys? Anything exciting?"

Jazmin frowned. Her brown eyes became hooded, and she stared listlessly at her computer screen. "Depositions. Always the depositions. Our stock in trade."

"Got a particularly boring one that's bogging you down at the moment?"

She shot PJ a stern look over the top of her gemmed glasses. "They are none of them boring. Some are disturbing, though. Desperate people do desperate things to other desperate people."

PJ nodded, her eyebrows tracing a deep V on her pale forehead. "I suppose so."

* * *

It was over an hour before Liam was done with his clients. In fact, when the consultation ended, PJ was surprised to see Alex and his mom come out. PJ stood as they neared the exit.

"Mrs. Tate! Alex. How are you?"

Alex smiled and buried his face in his mom's shoulder. At first Maija Tate didn't seem to recognize PJ. The woman blinked repeatedly, her head bobbing backward as if trying to flee her neck. She had small hazel eyes in a darkly tanned face and bottle-blond hair. She was taller than PJ—most people were—and heavyset. Today Maija wore a tight black sweater, dangling silver earrings, and jeans, and she had her hair pulled back into a tight bun.

"Oh. PJ Taylor. Nice to see you."

It was a canned response, uttered out of a sense of civility rather than any genuine pleasure.

"I'm sorry about the accident, but I'm glad Alex is okay." PJ looked Alex in his big hazel eyes that had lashes long enough to make any woman acutely jealous. He dropped his gaze to the floor and bleated faintly.

Alex's mom grabbed his arm and led him toward the door. "We're not saying anything about it. Come on, Alex."

Alex's face fell, and he made another goat-like grumble.

"Well, see you back at the Hills," PJ said as they left.

PJ turned her attention to Liam, who had just emerged from his office at the end of the hall. Instead of coming her way, he headed away from her, into the break room. PJ stood alone for a while, then headed over to Jazmin's counter. "So Liam's representing Alex and his mom? Why do they even need a lawyer?"

Jazmin pulled her movie-star glasses down her nose and peered at PJ over them. "Why does anyone need a lawyer? The police, if they are after you, they will get you."

PJ frowned. She stared at the countertop in front of Jazmin. "I thought it was an accident."

"I know; that's what you called it."

"What?"

"You said 'accident' from the beginning. But other people aren't so sure. Especially other people of the law enforcement variety."

"What else would it be?"

The women stared at each other for a couple of heartbeats. Then PJ gasped. "Jazmin. They're not saying Alex had anything to do with Chip Greene falling in the water, are they?"

The corners of Jazmin's lips turned downward. "I am afraid there is a real tragedy in the making here."

Liam's deep voice came from the mouth of the hall as he approached them. "Jazmin, are you finished with the depositions yet?"

"Oh, I will be shortly, sir." Jazmin blushed, a tinge of red touching the tops of her brown cheeks. She replaced her glasses and applied herself to her computer.

PJ turned toward Liam. He said, "Hello, PJ, my beautiful friend. How are you?"

He took PJ briefly in his arms, and they kissed on both cheeks. PJ was lost momentarily in his familiar aftershave, undertones of juniper and pine with a hint of mint. Memories of her time with Liam shot through her subconscious at the recognition of that aftershave, and she was flooded with a deep sense of nostalgia, of unrequited love and missed opportunity.

They had grown up together, and she had seen him transform from a scrawny, dirty-blond scamp with curious blue eyes and a chip on his shoulder into a strapping young man with an immovable sense of justice who wanted to dedicate his life to something of tangible good. Now he was thirty, like PJ, and working like a dog for the people of Indianapolis so they wouldn't be crushed under the weight of a legal system designed to uplift the haves at the expense of the have-nots. A system supported by endless fees and retainers and plea bargains, where money was freedom and no money meant jail.

PJ and Liam had been engaged ten years previously when Liam was a dedicated university student, burning himself out at both ends for his law degree. They had even made it to the altar, right to Peck Chapel on the university campus, where everything had gone wrong from the start. Of course PJ needed the cover of daylight, but relatives were flying in, and the earliest they could start the ceremony would be two in the afternoon on a cloudy March day. Everyone was late, including PJ. By the time the vows were being exchanged, the sun was angled terrifyingly low, and long shadows lit the stained glass images, patches of red, gold, and green falling on PJ's worried face at the altar. In retrospect, she figured she must have been completely out of her mind to accept Liam's proposal. At twenty, she was still under the impression she could somehow have half a normal life. These days, at thirty, she laughed at herself. How naive she had been.

The sun had dipped, the priest had droned on, the guests were still arriving, and right as the words "I do" were about to leave her lips, she felt the change coming and knew she had seconds to decide. Show everyone who she was or run—run full tilt, heels flying, down the aisle, out the side door, away from the chapel, and into the parking lot where Liam found her wedding dress behind a brown Camero. To him, it must have seemed she was shedding him, shedding their interrupted vows and the life they'd imagined together. Literally shedding his love and abandoning him, running naked through the campus, not to be found that night or for several days afterward until she appeared at his house in the rain, bawling and penitent, finally explaining she couldn't commit and should have never promised in the first place, but she wouldn't love anyone else.

His vast sense of good in the world was the only thing that saved PJ and kept Liam from slamming the door in her face or strangling her on the stoop. They cried together for hours, until she had to run away once again because sunset was coming. She spent weeks hating herself and cursing her gift. He spent weeks lost in studying, seeing no one, not even his horrified parents who had warned him about the capriciousness of orphans. Once abandoned, always to abandon, they had told him. Liam refused to believe this, even after it happened. His angst merged with the charitable nature of his soul until he saw them as one and the same: forgiveness to PJ was forgiveness to the world of unfortunates, and he would strive endlessly to help them until one day he would save them all and there would be no need for anyone to abandon anyone else ever again. At least, that was the twenty-year-old's hope. By thirty, Liam was more hardened, with a streak of gray in his darkening hair. He remained, however, a perpetual optimist, a fount of moral good, and one of the bulwarks of PJ's world.

She said, "How's Rose? And the kids?"

Liam had recovered, as had PJ. He had found a woman who did not jilt him at the altar and instead provided him with a warm home and three children, two boys and a cute little girl. He'd been waiting for a girl, and Annabeth was now almost two.

"Little Beth is a terror and drives her mom completely nuts. The girl rips up the carpets and destroys the boys' Lego towers so they'll scream when they get home."

PJ laughed. "That'll teach you the error of your ways."

"You mean the error of having kids so precious it makes my eyes water just to think about them?"

"That's the one."

He chuckled. "I'll take it. It's just a phase. She'll get over it."

"Yeah, I'm sure she'll be worse at three. Louder and stronger, too."

He snorted. "Probably. But it's lunchtime. Did you notice that?"

"I noticed."

"Let's hit the sandwich shop a couple of doors down. I would take you somewhere more special, but I've got another meeting at one, so I won't have time to drive anywhere."

* * *

They settled into a booth at the back of the shop near the restrooms where they had a bit of privacy. In spite of their past, they still fell into a sense of pair-hood when they were together, a sense of them against the world. Always choosing seating with the most privacy and the ability to watch their surroundings was lingering evidence of that.

PJ was wondering how to broach the subject of Alex when Liam said, "PJ, I've been meaning to talk to you about the Tate case."

PJ swallowed. "Me too."

"Okay, you first."

"Why does Alex even need you?"

Liam's hand went to his chin, and he rubbed it furiously. "What have you heard?"

"Not much. But I was there. I saw what happened. Chip Greene fell in of his own accord, and Alex almost died trying to save him."

Liam's eyes widened. "You were there?"

"Well, I was up the hill and some way south. But, that's what I thought I saw."

"Please tell me you have photo proof of that."

"I wish I did. I have nothing as of yet."

"Tell me what happened. From the beginning."

PJ told Liam her story about having light goggles and using them to become accustomed to moving around in the night. Then she reiterated that she saw Alex and Chip from a distance.

"Alex didn't push him," PJ said. "There was a shot, and I think it startled Chip, so he fell in. He dragged Alex in with him."

"Yet Alex managed to get out again."

"Mutt was with me. He ran over and pulled Alex from the water. Chip disappeared pretty fast."

"Where were you when Mutt was pulling Alex from the water? Did you call 911?"

As always, PJ realized there were holes a mile wide in her story. She was starting to think she should get some throwaway phones and teach her cat self to dial 911 on them. Hadn't she read that even if no one says anything, they can triangulate on the phone signal and the ambulances will come anyway? How she wished she'd had one that night. Instead of falling out of a tree and being washed away, she could have gotten some help. In all of her years of close scrapes and cat shenanigans, she'd never had anything to do with a death. Thieving teens or Peeping Janes were one thing; somebody actually dying was another.

PJ fidgeted with her water glass. "I didn't realize there was such a big problem. I got scared and went home, back to a safe place and the light."

Liam seemed lost in thought.

PJ said, "What?"

"Alex did seem to be talking about a big dog. I guess it was Mutt saving him that he meant. You know it's hard to get anything out of him."

"Why are you telling me this? Aren't you bound by privilege?"

"I got special permission from Alex's mom to use my judgment about what to tell you. You should know, though, that I won't tell you anything I think would hurt them if it got out."

"Of course not. But Alex didn't do anything wrong. Are they going to arrest him?"

"Not yet, but the police want to question him. We've had an initial session that didn't go well and we've got another appointment for tomorrow with your deputy friend."

"Vicky?"

"That's the one."

"How do you mean your questioning didn't go well?"

"Do you know Jake Tipton?"

"He's a detective in the Mayhap Police."

"Yes. Well, he seems to think the evidence shows Alex pushed Chip Greene into the water after Greene tried to shoot him with his pellet gun. They're trying to get Alex to confess and plead self-defense."

"But that's not what happened."

"PJ, tell me again what you saw."

PJ sighed. "I really didn't get a good enough look to be sure. But the shot that everyone heard wasn't from Chip. It came from the trailer park behind all of us."

"Are you sure?"

"I'm sure it didn't come from Chip's direction."

"And you're okay with testifying to all of this?"

Fear shot down PJ's spine. "Gosh. Do you think it'll come to that?"

"If it does, I'll have to subpoena you. You might be our only hope."

"This whole thing is crazy."

"Tell that to Jake and Vicky."

Their order number was called, and Liam got up to retrieve their sandwiches. When he came back, they ate in silence for several minutes.

PJ wanted desperately to change the subject. "Are you going to the cookout this weekend?"

Vicky and Curtis had a knack for inviting anyone in town at the center of any ongoing gossip or speculation. PJ figured that meant most of the major players in the recent incidents would be there. It might mean fireworks, which, in turn, would mean everyone tangential would definitely come, if for no other reason than the confrontation potential.

"Probably," Liam said. "I assume half the town will be there as usual?"

PJ chuckled. "I'm sure people are coming out of the woodwork and randomly suggesting they be invited. But, Vicky usually manages to keep it reasonable."

"Have you talked to Robert?"

"Yes. He wants Alex to be more forthcoming. He thinks keeping silent is hurting your appearances."

"Of course he'd say that. He's looking to arrest someone, not to help out an unfortunate autistic boy."

"I don't think you give Robert enough credit."

As far as PJ could remember, there had always been conflict between Robert and Liam, especially when she and Liam were an item. Robert had been like a father to PJ and seemed to take the job very seriously when vetting any potential suitors.

PJ always wondered at Robert's opposition to Liam. She secretly thought it arose from her brother's deeply denied knowledge of her cat-ness and a resulting subconscious desire to protect her secret from everyone, including himself. Although PJ and Liam had been friends since they could walk and had dated for two years before their ill-fated engagement, Liam didn't know about PJ's second life. Sometimes PJ wondered how on earth she'd managed to keep it a secret all this time. It seemed blindingly obvious to her—the slip-ups in speaking, the close calls. Yet, she supposed, it was so far out of everyone else's imagination that they couldn't see it, even if it was in front of their faces. She was just a woman with an odd phobia of the dark and a propensity for telling good yarns, that's all. Who would ever have thought any of that was because she was feline from sundown to sunup? No one. Especially not the two men closest to her in the world.

Liam huffed, breaking PJ from her reverie. "Good old Robert. When he's not pushing pencils, he's arresting special-needs teenagers."

"Wow, that's harsh."

Liam closed his eyes. "Sorry, PJ. That slipped out. I've been working a lot of overtime lately. The kids miss their dad, and it's hard on me too."

PJ noticed then the fine lines around his eyes that seemed to have sprung up since she'd seen him last. When he opened his blue eyes once more and looked at her, she could see a fatigue in them, a dampening of his usual joie de vivre. Was it possible a life devoted to pro bono work was capable of draining even Liam? PJ didn't want to think about that.

She patted the hand lying on the table. "It's okay. But you really need to take time for yourself too. And Rose and the kids."

"I know." He half smiled, and PJ's heart warmed.

"Is there anything I can do to help?"

"If you were to suddenly discover video of Chip's accident and Alex's rescue as it really happened, that'd be great. I mean, you usually have pictures of anything important in Mayhap."

"I'm not sure my sources will come through this time, but I can at least talk to Vicky and Jake and try to get them to see reason."

"Be careful, PJ. Those two might not ultimately be as friendly as you think they are."

9

Cookout

Vicky and Sheriff Curtis's cookout partially turned into a wake. Invitees were encouraged to wear black and the house was opened up to anyone who wanted to come pay their respects to the guest of honor, Phil Greene. Phil was Chip's half-brother and had come down from Wisconsin to see to his brother's effects. Phil wore a dark tartan shirt and black trousers, had a full beard and mustache, and generally seemed a much more jovial and personable man than his half-brother, in spite of being subdued due to the circumstances. PJ liked him immediately.

The usual ribs were accompanied by a large, generously apportioned buffet table and a dessert bar. PJ inhaled two servings of ribs, two plates of salad, and half a pie before Vicky cornered her and made her promise not to eat any more. PJ then switched to sweet iced tea and drank vast amounts to keep her complaining stomach full.

Clara found out Chip Greene's favorite color had, in fact, been green and insisted everyone at the wake don a green ribbon, corsage, necktie, or some other appropriate adornment. PJ wore her mother's emerald pendant earrings. Jake Tipton found PJ near the punch table, and although he was wearing a bright green ribbon on his lapel PJ thought his eyes were all the gem-like green he needed. She blushed at the thought. How could any man have such fantastic eyes?

"Beautiful earrings, PJ."

"Thanks."

"Lucky they didn't get stolen during your break-in."

"I know. But I hide my jewelry all over the house in odd places. My dad's ring was the most obvious one, near the top of the coffee grounds in the tin on the counter. These were... well, much better hidden. I guess I won't give away my other places. Unless you have a warrant." PJ flashed Jake a broad smile.

He laughed. "No such thing."

They watched Phil Greene playing foosball with Sheriff Curtis.

"Terrible thing, this," Jake said.

PJ stared at his somber profile. "Yes. Are you investigating it?"

He turned to her, his green eyes opaque. "Of course."

"Why?"

He blinked several times. "What?"

"Why do they have you investigating Chip Greene's drowning?"

"Because I'm a detective?"

PJ gave his arm a playful slap.

"Careful." He chuckled. "Assaulting an officer will get you in very serious trouble."

"Uh-huh. I mean, why are they having you investigate the drowning when it was clearly an accident?"

He stared at her for several moments. She became self-conscious and sucked back her entire glass of sweet iced tea in one go. She wished she had another piece of pie to hide behind.

Jake said at last, "You sound awfully sure about that."

PJ hesitated. She really didn't want to get into another discussion of how she was there. She knew her story was as thin as springtime ice. She hated all the half-truths her condition had her telling. She just hoped she could keep straight what she had told to whom.

"I just can't believe anyone's responsible for it. Especially Alex Tate."

"You don't think that boy hated Chip Greene like everyone else?"

"Hate is too strong a word. Chip was a jerk, but I can't imagine Alex doing anything intentionally."

"Hm." Jake focused on taking a bite from the plate he was carrying.

"What do you have against Alex, anyway?" PJ found herself staring at Jake with an odd feeling in her heart, suspicion mixed with doubt.

Jake sipped from the champagne glass he had sitting on the table beside them. "Someone witnessing something like someone falling into a raging river usually thinks to go get help."

PJ wasn't sure if Jake was talking about her or Alex. A chill passed down her spine. "What do you mean?"

"Wouldn't you call 911? I mean, if you saw someone fall into the water and drift away?"

"Uh." PJ noticed her hands were shaking. She took a deep breath and tried to quiet her telltale reactions. "Well, I guess I might try to help first."

"After calling 911, hopefully."

"I might not have a phone handy."

"The whole night, no 911 call."

"Alex is only fifteen. If he'd been thrashing around in the cold water and nearly lost his own life, maybe he was too freaked out—especially with his disability. He probably didn't understand enough to think right."

"I think Alex Tate understands more than anyone gives him credit for. He must not have told his mom about his predicament because I can only assume she would have had the wherewithal to call 911."

"Sometimes he can hardly talk. Plus, doesn't his mom work nights?"

"Not that night. Their truck was gone, but it was Trent, Alex's older brother, who took it."

"Oh."

Jake stared at the floor between them. "Nuts."

"What?"

"I'm sure I'm giving away some things I shouldn't. It's hard to remember you're just a civilian and not law enforcement, too. Somehow, the way people talk about you, I feel like you're more of a detective than I am."

"It's my cat eyes."

"What?"

"The yellow eyes." She pointed to her eyes. "My hypnotic cat eyes. I get people to tell me things."

He chuckled. "I guess so. What do you do with all these things people tell you?"

PJ smiled mischievously at him. "Sometimes I put them in my newspaper articles and get people in trouble."

"Aw, darn. I'm screwed."

* * *

After Jake left to greet some friends, PJ lifted a brownie from the dessert table and shoved it in her mouth.

"Hey, I told you no more food. You'll singlehandedly bankrupt us."

PJ started and wiped her mouth with her napkin. "Mgmph." She swallowed and cleared her throat. "I mean, yes, ma'am." She briefly saluted Vicky, who laughed.

"Looks like you and Detective Tipton are hitting it off."

PJ knew that was code for "tell me everything he said," but resisted. All she said was, "I guess so."

Vicky eyed her askance. "He's pretty cute."

"Does he have a girlfriend? Wife?" PJ asked.

"Not that I know of."

"Interesting. What's wrong with him?"

Vicky rolled her eyes. "You're never satisfied. If they're hooked up, they're off limits; if they're not, there's something wrong with them."

"I guess you're right. There's just as likely to be something wrong with them if they are hooked up as not. The world's a crazy place."

"There's something wrong with you too, girl, so don't always be the single kettle turning away all those pots."

Before PJ could answer that, a booming voice interrupted.

"Well, PJ, you staying out of trouble now?"

The sheriff came over and slung an arm around his wife, who elbowed him in the ribs. "Ow. Police brutality. You see how she treats me, PJ?"

"Poor man." PJ stuck out her tongue. Everyone laughed.

"That's my girl," Curtis said. "So did you get pics of the Greene murder or what?"

PJ scoffed. "Why would you think I have pictures of some random night-time event? And why are you calling it a murder?"

"It wasn't random. And it was right by your house. And it was big. Usually whenever something big is happening in town, we just wait until you send pictures of it. We don't even have to do our jobs. We just look at your pictures."

The three of them chortled amicably. Then the smile dropped from PJ's face. "Why is everyone calling it a murder?"

"You're right," Curtis said. "Technically the ME's report isn't back yet. Silly me."

"It wasn't a murder; it was an accident. I'm sure of it."

Sheriff Curtis nodded slowly. "Uh-huh. Sure. Well, we'll see."

"I don't get it. Chip fell in the water and unfortunately drowned. Alex even tried to save him."

"He didn't call 911."

"So I heard. But, that's not evidence of anything but a muddled state of mind."

Sheriff Curtis glanced over his shoulder. No one seemed to be paying attention to their conversation.

"The ME report isn't official yet, but I'll tell you, PJ. Keep it quiet."

"You know me. I'm the soul of discretion."

"Like mud is the soul of the Mississippi. But the body was moved."

PJ blinked repeatedly, trying to process what that meant. "What do you mean moved? Wasn't it found in the water? Of course it moved."

"No, moved, as in wherever he died didn't correspond to the evidence in the spot he was found in."

"I heard he was found by the bridge?"

"Way south of Stoker Hills where he went in. Yep."

PJ had known there must be something wrong with that. Before her own near-fatal trip through the water, she had seen him much farther north. But she didn't want to tell Sheriff Curtis that—at least not yet.

"None of this makes any sense."

"You're telling us," Curtis said. Vicky nodded.

"You're saying Alex moved Chip, too, as well as pushed him in? What did he do? Follow him down the river and then keep him underwater? I can't believe it."

Vicky said, "Why are you so bent on defending Alex Tate? Just because he's a fellow resident of Stoker Hills? You know people in that dang trailer park commit crimes by the dozen. Just think of his brother, Trent Tate. You got him on video stealing from your trailer, for heck's sake. And whenever we hear about users and gofers, guess where they're from?"

PJ frowned. "There's a couple hundred people in the Hills. There's bound to be some losers. The only difference between Stoker and somewhere like Wrenfield Downs is the good people of the Downs don't get convicted because they can afford much better lawyers." Wrenfield Downs was Mayhap's most elite neighborhood; the mayor himself lived amid its impeccable landscaping and imposing mansions.

Sheriff Curtis chortled. "You turning all socialist on us now? Maybe you should run an Occupy Main Street parade."

"Possibly I will."

"Don't encourage her, Curtis, for heaven's sake," Vicky said.

The sheriff walked away, chuckling and snuffling to himself as he went. "I don't need to encourage her. She encourages herself. Good old PJ."

* * *

After Vicky and Sheriff Curtis wandered off, PJ ambled around for a bit and then noticed her sister-in-law and niece sitting on couches in the living room. She went over and took up a place beside Nanci on the plush camel-colored sofa. Nanci, the wonderful girl, handed her a brownie.

"Here, Aunt PJ, I saved one for you. I know Deputy Vicky always tells you not to eat after a while, but you're always starving."

"Oh, you are a doll. Thanks, Nanci."

Nanci smiled, her amber-and-chestnut eyes sparkling. She hadn't inherited the intense yellow of her aunt's eyes, rather the darker brown-gold of her father's. PJ found her catlike anyway. It would serve Robert right, PJ thought, if his daughter turned into a cat. Would he deny what he saw with her? Would he turn his back on her for being too feline? PJ sincerely hoped not. And she harbored hopes for Nanci's fellow catness, in spite of hearing and detecting nothing that indicated the girl was other than naturally special. PJ's gift had started at puberty, at thirteen. Nanci was twelve and probably not quite there yet. PJ awaited the coming years with a mixture of apprehension and hope. Would she finally have a counterpart? Or would poor Nanci continue to lead a normal life? PJ didn't know which she was hoping for more.

To her sister-in-law, Didi, PJ said, "Is Robert around?"

"Somewhere. I think he might be schmoozing the mayor in the kitchen."

"The mayor's here?"

"Sure is. As well as everyone else, it seems." Indeed, the living room was packed. Aside from the space Didi and Nanci had carved out on the sofas, it was standing room only.

"Robert says you think Chip Greene's death was an accident," Didi said.

Nanci said, "I think it was an accident, too."

Her mother shushed her. "Nanci, you think whatever PJ thinks. We all know that."

"No, really, I do," Nanci insisted. "I've been investigating, and it's definitely an accident. A hundred percent."

PJ turned to her niece. "You've been investigating?"

Didi said, "She's started a detective club with her friend Bridget."

"Interesting."

"Yeah!" Nanci said. "It's so cool. I use that big magnifying glass you gave me when I was ten, Aunt PJ. We were walking around the ravine, and we found clues near Bridget's house."

PJ's cat sense tingled along her scalp. "What'd you find?"

"Well, Bridget found you that morning, remember?"

"Oh. Uh, right." PJ had no idea how she'd explain that. She looked at Didi sheepishly, but Didi was studying an imaginary speck on her skirt.

"Wasn't that weird? Did you see anything?"

"Not really."

Nanci's face fell. "That's too bad. We were hoping you saw the same thing that we did."

"And what's that?" PJ asked.

"We found a shoe!"

"A shoe? Where?"

"On the other side of the water, a ways north toward Stoker Hills. It was a hundred and sixteen steps from where Bridget found you," Nanci added confidently.

"What kind of shoe?"

"It looked like a man's loafer, and it was almost buried in the mud. If I didn't have my magnifying glass, I'm sure I wouldn't have seen it. Do you think it had something to do with that man who drowned? It can't be just a coincidence."

"I hope you didn't touch the shoe."

"Oh, we were very careful to leave it alone, just like real detectives. You know they have to keep away and let the CSI people handle everything like that—at least that's what Dad says. Plus we didn't want to dig in the icky mud. So we set up some crime scene tape around it."

"Crime scene tape? Did you take that from your dad?"

"Well, it's not real crime scene tape. We borrowed some yellow electrical tape from Bridget's dad."

"Did you tell your dad about the shoe?"

"We sure did. He was very proud. He made me an honorary agent. I'm Junior Special Agent Taylor now. It is the coolest thing in the history of the universe. I bet we could get him to make you an honorary special agent too, if you want, Aunt PJ. Do you want to join my club?"

Didi dissolved into giggles.

"I'm way too old," PJ said. "I'd just slow you girls down."

* * *

Robert was in the kitchen when PJ found him. The room was huge with infinite counters, two breakfast nooks, chrome appliances, and a long breakfast bar. Robert was propped against one of the breakfast bar stools, listening to the mayor and Sheriff Curtis converse. PJ closed up to him and whispered near his ear, "Can we talk?"

He peeled himself away from the others and followed PJ to a small reading area overlooking the backyard, with two chairs and a bookcase. Fortunately, the space was unoccupied. They sat and Robert leaned toward her, hands folded together and elbows propped on his knees.

"PJ, is there something you want to confess to me?"

"Uh. I wouldn't say confess."

His golden-brown eyes shone in the daylight of the sliding glass doors beside him. Occasionally people came or went through the doors, occluding those inquiring, clever eyes when their shadows passed over Robert.

"Okay, chat then. Let's say you wanted to chat."

"I guess you've talked to Nanci and Bridget."

He nodded slowly.

"They're investigating the drowning, I gather."

He nodded slowly again.

PJ sighed. "Can you chat too? It's not only me here. You know I hate talking to a vacuum."

Robert unfolded his hands and rubbed them up and down his thighs. "Nanci found a shoe, it seems. We have the crime lab looking at the area."

"Is it Chip's?"

"Too early to say."

"Let's pretend it is. What do you think it means?"

"What do you think it means?"

"I asked you first."

"PJ, if you want something from me, you have to give first. What in the heck were you doing washed up naked there that morning?"

Fear shot through PJ. How could she possibly explain? She didn't have a ready story cooked up because she had forgotten that she would need one. She'd been so busy running around trying to come to terms with Chip's drowning that she'd completely forgotten how deeply she had to justify her role in that night's events.

She crimsoned. "It's embarrassing."

"Try me. I'm your brother. I raised you from a teenager. You can't embarrass me any more than you probably already have at some point."

"Well, you know I have to wear those light goggles when I'm out."

"Yes. And I gather they make it so you can't see very well, since you couldn't really see what happened with Alex and Chip."

PJ cleared her throat. "Well, no. Anyway, I, uh, slipped."

"You slipped?"

"Yes. I fell into the river too. Just like Chip."

Robert ran his fingers through his hair. "Jeez, PJ. You could have been killed. Why were you naked when you washed up?"

"I just had my robe on. I was only investigating because of the shot. My robe must have fallen off and washed away."

Robert sighed. "PJ, you're not making this easy. Every time I talk to you, your story changes. How am I supposed to defend you if you don't tell me everything?"

"Defend me? Defend me how? From who?"

A large man carrying a plate bulging with pastries slid open the door and exited, closing the door behind him.

Robert laced his fingers together and tapped his thumbs. "People are talking. It's just a matter of time before you're going to have to get your story straight."

PJ felt her neck and face heat up. She said clearly, in a low voice, "Well, Robert, you know I turn into a cat nightly. I witnessed the whole thing but fell into the river trying to save Chip and woke up the next morning by Bridget's house with no memory of what happened in the water. Of course I don't have clothes when I'm a cat, so I have none when I turn back into a human either."

Robert closed his eyes. "Very funny."

Now PJ could always and forever afterward say she tried. She had tried to tell Robert the truth, but it was beyond his powers of imagination. Now, she felt, she could say that whatever she made up was completely justified. When the truth was "impossible," better to make up something improbable since that's what people could believe.

"Okay, fine, it's part of my therapy."

"What?" Robert's eyes snapped open.

"My therapy. Getting adjusted to being out in the night. That's why I was out there. I'm supposed to start with ten minutes or so and work my way up. I happened to be out there during the ten minutes with Alex, Chip, and the shot. I have to say, I was so stunned by the whole thing, and so freaked out by the noise of the shot, that I fell into the river. My robe got lost, as I told you, and other than that I don't remember anything until I woke up with Bridget poking me the next morning."

"That's your story?"

PJ noted the timbre of Robert's voice was far more skewed toward belief than when she told him the actual truth mere moments ago.

She smiled. "I know. I feel stupid, but what can I say? It was the world's worst timing. How was I to know that at the exact time I'm poking around for ten minutes with those stupid light goggles on there would be a town-shattering accident? I've been out there trying to get used to the night for weeks, and no one's ever noticed, and I've never been washed downstream. Then the other night, bam! Everything goes all wonky."

Robert had his eyes closed again and was rubbing his forehead. "How am I supposed to tell this to the sheriff? The police? They'll think we've both gone off the deep end. Can you at least get Doc Fred to confirm your so-called therapy?"

"You know it doesn't work that way. He's bound to silence."

PJ had no clue what Doc Fred would say if Robert did ask him. But she'd sent more than one questioner his way before and so far her luck had held. From the rumors, she thought Doc Fred seemed as eager to pretend they had a therapeutic relationship as she was. She supposed he might be grateful for the publicity of treating the famous town nutball, PJ Taylor. If Mayhap were Beverly Hills, they'd probably have a line of swag devoted to their mutual cause and sell fifty-dollar rhinestone-studded T-shirts to movie stars.

"Great," Robert said.

"So back to the shoe."

He glared at her. "The shoe?"

"Yes. The one Nanci and Bridget found? The one they cordoned off with yellow electrical tape? The one you just said was inconclusive yet?"

He laughed. "As usual, you know everything, don't you?"

"Well, in addition to being a cat and running around at night with light goggles, I'm a psychic, don't you know."

Robert's laughing turned into swelling snorts. "You're too much, PJ. I can't take it."

"You know you should keep yourself calm, Robert. It's kind of unseemly for a man your age to be screaming with laughter like a little girl."

That, naturally, made him laugh even harder. The guffaws meant he could hardly breathe and barely made any sounds; his whole body was wracked with convulsions. PJ couldn't help it; she also had to laugh uproariously, trying to suppress it so she wouldn't fill the house with screeching hyena-like cries.

The siblings shook together with laughter in the corner for several moments, but then a plate shattered, stopping their antics short.

"—enough of you people!" a woman yelled.

Both Robert and PJ got up quickly and stepped back through the archway dividing the reading nook and the kitchen. They saw Doc Fred and his wife, Minerva, restraining an old woman. The woman's dark face was nearly purple, and her eyes bugged out.

"You're all against us. You're all against him! The malpractice insurance is killing us! Killing us! You come at night to kill us in our sleep! You come from the water to kill us!"

The group around the old woman was silent and dismayed. Doc Fred and his wife dragged her toward the exit. Her screams degenerated into profanity, and PJ could hear her yelling all the way through the foyer out into the front yard. Out the front window, she watched Doc Fred and Minerva pile the woman into their car and drive away. The rest of the party went on, as if in unspoken agreement to pretend nothing had happened.

Robert stood beside PJ, watching the Nortons' car drive away. "Who was that?" PJ asked.

"I think that was Doc Fred's mother," he answered.

"What's wrong with her?"

"Dementia, seems like."

"Poor Doc Fred."

Robert looked meaningfully at PJ. "He's a psychiatrist, not a miracle worker. Some things just can't be cured."

PJ realized he was alluding to her as well as the old woman. She stared at the floor. What could she say? There was nothing to say. She had her story now, and she would need to stick to it. She remained silent for several moments before rejoining the party with a subdued demeanor for the rest of the afternoon.

10

Funeral

Chip Greene's funeral was held the following day, a brilliantly sunny Sunday. The air was crisp but held the promise of summer to come. PJ wasn't invited, but she read the schedule in the paper, so she walked out to the cemetery to see if she could catch the interment. Mayhap's Memorial Cemetery was only a mile and a half from Stoker Hills, along Mayhap Road, past the bridge where Chip's body was found and around a long bend.

When PJ got to the cemetery, she saw some activity in the eastern quarter up a hill. She took up a place at a discrete distance and watched the scene. So far, only the gravediggers were there, preparing the hole for Chip's casket. After a few minutes, a familiar person joined her.

"Hello, Robert."

Her brother nodded. "They're done at the church. They should be coming here shortly."

"Were you at the service?"

"No. It was private. Only Phil and a couple of Chip's drinking buddies seemed to be in attendance."

PJ turned to Robert. He was wearing a dark suit with a light blue shirt and tie. He had on mirrored sunglasses that reflected the big pink flowers of a nearby magnolia. A gentle breeze stirred the tree, and the flowers waved at them as if to say hello.

"Will they mind that we're here for the interment?" PJ asked.

"It's a free country. They can't close the cemetery to the public."

PJ and Robert were silent for a few moments. The gravestones arrayed before them were somber and still in the afternoon sun.

PJ said, "Have there been any developments? Did you figure out who the shoe Nanci found belongs to?"

"It's Sunday, PJ. Things are slow. We'll just have to be patient."

PJ considered everything she knew about the fateful night when Chip was washed away in the raging water. She had far more questions than answers. "I just don't get it," she mused aloud.

"What don't you get?"

"For starters, I don't get why Detective Tipton thinks Alex pushed Chip."

"There was a healthy amount of mud around the scene, PJ. The footprints seemed to tell that story."

"What about the pistol you guys found in the water? Chip's pellet gun? At the most, I'd say Alex was probably defending himself."

"The pellet gun was inconclusive. There was no ammunition inside, but we couldn't tell if it had been recently fired since it was in the water."

"What about the shot everyone heard?"

"You were there. Did you see Chip shoot the gun?"

"From where I was, it didn't look like anyone had a gun. And the shot seemed to come from behind me, in the trailer park, not the ravine."

"A loud noise is often hard to pinpoint, especially with echoes."

"I'm not even sure it wasn't a tree branch breaking."

"Two of your neighbors called 911 about it. They seemed pretty sure it was a shot."

"Well, maybe someone else was there, shooting at Chip and Alex."

Robert frowned. "Someone else? Do you have any basis to think that?"

PJ remembered Mutt smelling cigarette smoke. Mutt had been sure it belonged to the short boy from the thefts. "I think I smelled cigarette smoke. From the direction of the Hills."

Robert rubbed his forehead. "Now you smelled smoke. PJ, why does your story constantly change? How can anyone believe you?"

"Well, it was all a jumble. And I did take a turn through the water. Maybe I hit my head. It's coming back to me in pieces."

"All right, so you smelled cigarette smoke. It could have been anyone. Perhaps one of the neighbors who called 911 was out in his yard smoking."

"Who's the second boy?"

"What?"

"In the break-in video, I saw Trent Tate and another boy. Who is he?"

"I'm not at liberty to say."

"Oh, come on, Robert. How am I supposed to piece things together if you won't help me?"

Robert was silent.

"Fine," PJ said. "But every time I see him, he seems to be smoking. What if he was there?"

"That's quite a leap."

"Well, when people are asking them questions about the thefts, I think they should also be asked if they were there Saturday night when Chip went in the water."

Robert stared at PJ. His mirrored eyes were opaque in the sunlight.

"And anyway," PJ said, "why haven't I heard back on the thefts? Surely the video gave enough evidence to arrest Trent, or at least search his trailer or something."

"Or something."

"What does that mean?"

"PJ, it's not that simple. For starters, Detective Tipton has been distracted by the whole Greene business. For finishers, I don't know why he hasn't moved on the thefts."

"Great. Meanwhile, either Trent or that short boy are pawning Dad's ring somewhere."

At the entrance to the cemetery, cars started to arrive, led by the hearse. The procession was short, only four cars total, and wound its way toward the open grave that had been prepared.

"So have you thought of anything else?" Robert asked.

PJ stared at the nearest headstone. A beetle was making its way up the side. "The shoe bothers me," she said.

"Back to that darn shoe."

"Well, Nanci said she found it about a hundred paces north from where Bridget found me the next morning. That's about where I fell in."

"You know this how? Have you been poking around back there?"

"Well of course I have."

Robert huffed. "Of course you have. And what bothers you about that shoe so much?"

The cars stopped at the top of the hill, and Chip's friends got out of their cars. The back of the hearse opened, and PJ could make out the casket, Chip's final carriage.

"Well, I think I saw Chip."

"You mean in the water?"

"No, on the side. Before I slid into the water, I think I saw him across from me."

"That makes no sense, PJ. How long was it between when you saw him fall in and when you fell in?"

"I was stumbling around for a while, blinded by the light goggles."

"And your story changes once again. Damn it, PJ."

"Well, I can't help what I saw. I could swear Chip was on the other bank from me when I fell in. And I thought he moved. So he was still alive."

"This is big, PJ. This is huge. If he washed up between when he went in and where he was found, then how did he get back in the water? Was the creek raging so much that it would have dragged him from the side?"

"No, if Chip was where I think he was, he would have needed help to get back in the water."

"You realize what you're saying, PJ."

"I'm saying that Alex didn't do it."

Robert sighed heavily. Meanwhile, up on the hill, Chip's ragtag group of drinking buddies carried his casket uncertainly to the grave. PJ saw Phil Greene, dressed in full Scottish formal, kilt and everything. His plaid was navy with green lines, and he carried a bagpipe.

"Wow, look at that," PJ said.

Robert turned to face the interment. Both of them watched as Phil took a couple of puffs on the bagpipe. After a moment, the sound of the warming-up pipes came to them as a series of broken wheezes. Shortly Phil's expertise took over, and "Amazing Grace" floated toward them on the chilly air. Both Robert and PJ listened in silence. PJ always wondered how anyone could make it through "Amazing Grace" on the bagpipes without crying. She couldn't. Tears streaked down her cheeks. Robert glanced her way, no evidence of grief across his face.

"Are you all right?" he asked.

PJ wiped her eyes with her fingers. "Funerals always remind me of Mom and Dad."

"I know. Me too."

"Then why aren't you crying?"

Robert didn't answer. As the last refrain from the pipes died away, PJ saw Chip's casket had been lowered into the grave. Chip's friends split off from the pastor and wandered back to their cars, looking a little dazed from the whole thing. Phil stayed behind to talk to the pastor.

"I guess that's it," PJ said.

Robert looked around the area. "How did you get here, PJ? I didn't see your car."

"I walked."

"Want a ride back home?"

"No, you go on. I want to be by myself."

11

Arrested

Monday morning PJ returned twenty minutes before sunup and pushed her way into her trailer through the cat door she'd had cut into her front door. She had just transformed and changed into pajamas and was about to lie down when someone pounded on her door. She opened it to find Maija Tate frantic and flushed.

"PJ, come quick! They're taking Alex. You have to help him!"

"What?"

"Get ahold of Liam and tell him to meet us at the municipal building."

PJ followed Maija in a rush back to her trailer. It was a single-wide with an addition built at right angles off the back for Trent's bedroom.

Mutt was on their heels, barking.

"Mutt, hush," PJ said.

Mutt sat and waited several feet away from the marked SUV in front of the Tates' trailer. PJ's heart sank when she saw who had come to arrest Alex—it was Jake. He stood with two other uniformed officers in front of a patrol car. Alex was sitting in the back seat, head bowed. PJ thought she heard soft bleating through one of the cruiser's open windows.

PJ cornered Detective Tipton near his SUV. "Jake, what happened? What are you doing?"

"Hey, PJ."

Mutt had inched closer to the SUV and was now a paw's length from Henry, who was shut in the back. They exchanged barks and growls.

"Mutt, heel," PJ said.

"Heinrich, platz!" Jake said.

"What's that?" PJ asked.

"Oh," Jake said. "It's German. That's what Henry—or rather Heinrich, actually—understands."

"Oh, nice."

"Uh-huh. My pronounciation is pretty bad, but Heinrich doesn't seem to mind."

"Well, you're his master."

"Yep."

The two officers standing nearby got into their cruiser and started it. Maija followed them out of the area in her red pickup, sending up a spray of gravel in her wake.

"Where are they taking him?" PJ asked Jake.

"Booking."

"I'll need to call Liam and get him to meet Alex and Maija there."

"Hm. Better get on that."

"I can't believe you actually arrested Alex. How can the DA possibly think there's enough evidence to try this? It's crazy."

Jake looked at his watch. "CSI should be here soon so we can search the trailer. We can kill two birds with one stone."

"What do you mean?"

"Well, our warrant includes the entire trailer. We can search for stolen goods as well. Perhaps Alex's brother, Trent, left some of his goodies lying around as evidence. Like your dad's ring, for example."

"Oh. That would be great. When would I get it back?"

"It would probably be a while. We'd have to use it as evidence in any case against Trent."

"Why are you just now getting to Trent?"

"We didn't get a warrant on your video evidence alone."

"What? How can that be?"

Jack shifted from foot to foot. "Well, Trent dropped the cat statue. And, frankly, it looked like a setup."

PJ's scalp crawled with fear and indignation. "A setup?"

"It looked as if the boys were enticed to go into your trailer. Especially since on the video you can't tell if they got away with anything. You can't see the ring, PJ."

"Yes you can, if you look closely."

"Well, the judge looked closely and disagreed."

PJ was saddened by Jake's matter-of-factness. Had she said or done something to put him off? He'd been warm at the cookout but now seemed made of ice. She bit her lip in lieu of snarking at him.

Jake checked his watch again. "Are you doing anything for lunch, PJ?"

PJ's eyes widened. Was he asking her out? "Uh, no, not at the moment."

"How about meeting me? I'd like to talk to you some more."

"Sure. Where?"

"The Village Grille? It's right on Main Street."

"I know where it is. That's one of my favorite places."

"Okay, good. See you there at twelve-thirty then."

* * *

After she left Jake, PJ went to her trailer and called Liam. He was at home in Mayhap, so it wouldn't take him long to get to the municipal building and meet Maija and Alex. PJ was mollified that at least she could call Liam to help, even if she couldn't do anything for Alex herself.

Afterward, PJ applied herself to the problem of her waterlogged camera. She figured since it had been a full week, its interior should be sufficiently dry by now to try to retrieve its contents. She carefully put it together and hooked it up to her computer. At first, she couldn't get the camera's internal flash drive to work at all. But after several minutes of trying different settings and carefully readjusting the connection, she managed to get a couple of files off her camera. It seemed so testy, though, that she knew she'd have to get rid of it. She had a back-up camera, but it was bigger and more bulky, so she didn't like to wear it. She'd just have to order a new and improved model, even smaller and thinner than the one that was now broken.

The files she retrieved weren't much help. She had been running when the camera was filming, so the images were jerky and nearly unrecognizable. She did see Alex and Chip standing together at the edge of the water. The next shot that was presentable was Chip flailing around in the water and Alex reaching for him. Alex's heavy tote bag unbalanced him, and he splashed into the water's edge. Then the clip ended. The only other footage that seemed intact consisted of a couple of frames of night sky through the branches of the trees as PJ tried to cross the river toward Chip. She was howling on the clip, and the effect was particularly eerie. She supposed she could save the video for Halloween, but other than that it was useless.

She sat back and sighed heavily. She knew her footage wouldn't help Alex. When the boy stumbled into the river, he had his arms out, and if you were already of that opinion, you might say Alex was pushing Chip. PJ knew what she had seen that night, though. It didn't happen that way. She decided it was best to keep the footage she did have to herself.

Before she closed the encrypted directory where she kept her videos, she decided to watch the video she'd taken of Trent and the short boy breaking into her trailer. She couldn't tell which of them had picked the lock on her front door, but it went so fast that whoever did it was surely well practiced. It almost looked as though the boys had a key to her trailer. The video cut out, and PJ opened the second half. In it, the boys emerged from her trailer, Trent clearly holding the cat figurine and the short boy holding his hand out boasting about the ring on his finger. PJ paused the recording and enlarged the short boy's hand. A fuzzy block on the second-to-last finger of his right hand was all she could make out. Yet she knew she had seen the class ring clearly the night of the theft. Apparently her cat eyes were better than the camera. She could see why the judge had opted to give the boys the benefit of the doubt. After Mutt scared them and Trent dropped the figurine, it looked as if the boys had gotten away with nothing. Yet something about the video was making PJ's cat-sense tingle. She had to watch the part where Mutt chased the boys three more times before she realized what it meant.

The short boy's arm had jerked when Mutt barked. It almost looked as if he were flicking something off his fingers. When PJ stopped the footage and magnified it to maximum, she could almost make out a small bit of silver flying through the air, seeming to originate at the short boy's out-flung hand.

PJ went outside. She crouched in the gravel near the stoop of her trailer and ran her hands along the uneven rocks. Slowly, she inched forward, running her hands over the pebbles, looking carefully at every inch within several yards of the stoop.

The sun had ascended almost to mid-sky when she finally found a metal object in the gravel a few feet from the stoop. The dulled surface of the ring almost didn't distinguish it from the gray and white rocks around it.

"Well, I'll be," PJ said out loud.

Her dad's ring.

As she stared at it, on her hands and knees and covered with dust, a deep voice behind her said, "What'd you find?"

She jumped to her feet. "Jeez, Robert. You startled me. Don't do that."

"PJ, I drove up and everything. You were so intent you didn't hear me. I've been standing here watching you for nearly five minutes. What were you looking for? What did you find?"

She unfurled her hand and showed him.

"Dad's ring. You found that just now?"

"Yup. Right there." She pointed slightly away from her feet.

"Imagine that. How'd you think to look for it?"

"The video. When Mutt chased the boys, Trent dropped what he was carrying. I thought it wasn't a stretch to think the other boy dropped his ill-gotten gains too. Plus, I sent the video to the police. Didn't they give you a copy?"

"PJ, I'm FBI. I'm after the big, bad drug dealers, not some small-time thieves."

"Even if they're one and the same?"

"What?"

"Trent is one of their runners, as far as everyone says."

"You know, that is what everyone says. But those are rumors. I can't arrest someone based on rumors."

"Well, at least I got Dad's ring back."

PJ handed it to Robert, who put it on his right ring finger. He held up his hand. "What do you think?"

"It suits you. Fits perfectly too."

"Uh-huh." He took it off and handed it back to PJ.

"So, Robert, are you here for any particular reason, other than to model Dad's ring and startle the crap out of me?"

"I'm here with a warning. Not that you ever listen to me."

PJ frowned. "A warning?"

"You've been hanging around Jake Tipton, right?"

"More like he's been hanging around with me. We're supposed to have lunch today." PJ looked up at the bright sun, which was almost directly overhead. "Very soon, in fact."

"Well, maybe you should think about canceling that."

PJ's eyes narrowed to slits. "Why on earth would I do that?"

"He's not the one for you, PJ."

"Oh. I get it. Mr. Big Brother comes to warn Miss Little Sister about the rough, bad boyfriend, right? Is there any man alive who would pass your tests for me?"

"Probably. But Jake is not him."

"You know you're going to have to give me more than that or I'll laugh at you right now. And maybe elope."

"For your sake, I sincerely hope you don't."

"Okay, why not? Is he too cute? Too nice? Too cop?"

Robert sighed. "Be reasonable, PJ. It might be that I've heard things you haven't. I am FBI, as you alway say, and it's possible I know him professionally and a heck of a lot better than you do."

"Fine. So give me some specifics. What should I be worried about?"

Robert rubbed the back of his neck. "It's heresay as of right now."

"So tell me."

"I really shouldn't. But your eyes—they're almost hypnotic. No wonder you manage to get everyone to spill the beans to you."

"Is that a compliment? You're just filled with sibling love today."

"I draw the line at rumors and innuendo. I hate repeating that stuff."

"Or maybe you just don't think I'll believe you."

Robert stared at her. PJ stared back. He dropped his gaze first.

"Fine, PJ. I think Jake is out to arrest you for the Stoker Hills thefts. Or at least for entrapment of Trent and his friend."

PJ's mouth dropped open, and she gaped at him, managing only to stammer an unintelligible syllable or two.

"Uh-huh. That's kind of what I thought your reaction would be. But it could be worse."

"W-worse? How could it get worse than that?"

Robert sighed. He rubbed his chin vigorously. He said nothing.

PJ felt like she'd been punched. "What? What could be worse?"

Robert straightened up to his full height and tucked his thumbs into his belt. He faced PJ full on.

"PJ, he might also be gunning for you for the Greene murder."

* * *

A few minutes after Robert left, PJ stomped around her trailer, talking in angry tones to herself.

"Darn it, Robert. Now you've gone and made me completely crazy right before my lunch with Jake. Jealous bastard."

She caught her reflection in her bedroom mirror.

"But what if he's right? What if I'm about to get sent up by a bad cop?"

She stared at her ashen, indignant face. Her shoulders drooped, and the dress she was holding hung limp in front of her.

"This is ridiculous. I'll just be careful, that's all. Jake's not a monster. Plus, I always have to be very careful anyway. How is this different?"

PJ dressed quickly in a gold shift dress that set off her eyes and emerald jewelry: a necklace, earrings, and a gorgeous pewter-and-emerald bracelet. It was probably the cat in her, but she was nuts about sparkly, shiny jewels. She had them in every color of the rainbow, hidden in all the nooks and crannies of her trailer. If Trent or his friend had known about all the bling PJ had out of sight, they would never have left with a figurine and a single ring. At the door, PJ grabbed a coordinating silver clutch purse and strappy sandals. Then she left to walk the half mile to Main Street to meet Jake.

The Village Grille was crowded, but Jake had thought to make a reservation and they ended up in a cozy corner near the back. The decor was pub-like, with dark wood and English-themed knickknacks. Their table was a picnic table with comfortable warping where their seats were. A waitress in jeans and a dark green T-shirt came to take their order. After they chose their meals, they handed the menus to the waitress, and she walked away to get their drinks. PJ had ordered ginger ale and Jake only water.

Jake silently watched PJ while they waited. If PJ had whiskers as a person, they would have been tingling furiously under his gaze. As it was, a faint pink tinge spread over her pale cheeks.

"Beautiful jewelry," Jake said at last. "You always seem to have the nicest pieces."

"Yes, these are from Lamont's. It's only two doors down from us." PJ gestured vaguely in the direction of the jewelry store on Main Street that was near the Village Grille. "Lucy is a friend of mine and gets me the nicest pieces. Whenever something colorful or sparkly comes in, she calls me for first dibs."

"So you spend all of your hard-earned freelance cash on shinies?"

PJ contemplated him, her amber eyes curious. "You really haven't heard all the gossip about me, have you?"

He smiled. "Nope. Why don't you fill me in?"

The waitress dropped off their drinks. PJ sipped her ginger ale through the straw.

"Well," she said, "I'm an heiress."

"Independently wealthy?"

PJ laughed. "Not by a long shot. But I have what my parents left me invested, and the income keeps me in baubles like these." She waved her arm, and the bracelet jumped and jingled, the emeralds scintilating in the overhead light.

"I see. So you live beneath your means."

"What?"

"You live in a trailer park. I gather you don't have to."

"I like Stoker Hills. It's home. Plus, I have everything I need."

"Well, it's a good thing Trent didn't know the rumors about you then."

"What do you mean?"

"They didn't look very hard for goodies when they went into your trailer. You only lost a figurine and a ring."

"Oh." PJ blushed. "About the ring."

Jake's green eyes were suddenly intent. "Yes?"

"I found it outside my stoop in the gravel. It must have fallen off the boy's finger when Mutt startled him."

"You found the ring?"

"Yes. Just this morning. My brother was there. He saw me find it."

Jake blinked several times before saying anything. "I guess that explains why we haven't found it among the treasures in Trent's room."

"Oh, did you search the Tate trailer? Did CSI finally get there?"

"We're still in the process of searching it. But when I left, we hadn't found any ring like you described."

"Well, no need to look for it anymore."

"Yes, I guess not."

Their orders came. PJ had a full side of ribs with a side of prawns, and Jake had a steak. When the waitress retreated, Jake said, "Wow, you really know how to eat. For a girl, that is."

PJ's eyes narrowed. Then she noticed the mirth in Jake's green eyes and chuckled. "Yes. A ravenous girl."

He laughed. "Good. I like a woman with an appetite."

PJ flashed him her most winning smile. He reciprocated in kind, and she almost melted into a puddle of desire right there in the booth.

They ate in silence for some time. Jake's steak was large and accompanied by onion rings. PJ's meal was heapingly huge, especially with extra sides of corn bread and potato salad.

During a pause in eating, Jake said, "So you have receipts for all the jewelry in your trailer, right?"

PJ put her fork down and finished chewing her mouthful. "What kind of question is that? Of course I do. Do I need them?"

Jake frowned. "I'm not sure."

"What's that supposed to mean? Do you think I stole my jewelry?"

"I don't think you're a petty thief, PJ."

PJ noted that wasn't a ringing endorsement. "But?"

Jake was silent. He cut a slice of steak, and PJ noticed his face had taken on a distinctly sullen demeanor.

PJ said, "Well?"

Jake folded his piece of steak into his mouth and chewed for a while. After he swallowed, he said, "Well, I'm not sure you're not the ringleader."

PJ's jaw dropped.

"You're kidding."

"That's what I wanted to talk to you about."

PJ placed her utensils on the side of her plate and stared at Jake. "You can't honestly believe anything like that."

"Think about it, PJ. You're the one with the video footage of the so-called thefts. But it's useless footage. Did you want us to chase our tails?"

PJ swallowed. "I don't think I should say any more."

"You're not under arrest or anything. I just wanted to talk about it. You know, casually."

PJ stared at her half-eaten plate of her favorite foods. Unfortunately, she had completely lost her appetite. How stupid was she? This wasn't a date. Jake wanted to pump her for information about imagined crimes she was committing.

"I don't think I'm hungry anymore."

"Aw, PJ, don't be like that. All I want is information."

"What kind of information?"

"Where were you the nights of February 12 and 16?"

PJ's shock came to a fine point. She felt a growing rage under her collarbone. How could she possibly explain? She couldn't have been stealing anything on those nights last month because she was a cat. She fidgeted with her fingers in her lap.

"I'm not saying anything more without Liam, Jake."

"Oh. Liam. The great savior of Stoker Hills." Jake shoveled another bite of steak into his mouth and chewed.

PJ stood to leave. "Sorry, Jake. I have to go. I'll pay for my own meal on my way out."

He stayed seated, concentrating on his meal. "I figured you might. Just don't leave town, okay?"

12

What Kitten Saw

That evening, PJ was sitting on her stoop with Mutt half in and half out of his doghouse. The sun had set and lit the sky behind them in dark streaks of apricot and fuchsia. The weather had turned chilly.

Both of them gawked as a young black cat strolled onto the lot, gingerly stepping amid the gravel of PJ's driveway.

PJ called, *Hello there.*

The kitten looked up at them. *Oh. Hi there.*

PJ recognized the kitten as the one with the infected eye she'd seen previously. The poor cat kept the eye closed, and it was obviously smarting.

Wait a minute, PJ said when the kitten made as if to leave the lot. *What's your name?*

The kitten turned and came closer, sitting near the bottom of the stoop and contemplating PJ and Mutt in turn. *Name?* he said.

Yes. Like, I'm PJ, and this is Mutt. PJ waved her head in Mutt's direction. The little cat nodded at both of them.

I don't think I have a name. At least not a human-given one.

Everyone has a name. Why don't you?

I'm a stray. No one wants me.

PJ waggled her whiskers. *You don't have to be a stray. My friend Clara is right down the road, and she takes everyone. Free food, free medical care, and a warm lightbox to sleep in.*

I know. The other cats told me. But I'm happy being free. If humans don't need me, why would I need them? Do you know any squirrels?

PJ sniffed loudly. *Those rodents? No way. They're food.*

Mutt barked in agreement.

Well, a couple are my friends. Click and Clack.

Okay, PJ nodded. *What do the squirrels call you then?*

Kitten.

Well then, that's your name. Nice to meet you, Kitten.

The small black cat eyed Mutt cautiously. *You're not going to eat my friends, are you?*

* * *

Later, Mutt, PJ, and Kitten sat in the ravine near where the waters had taken Chip Greene for the second time. The crime scene tape had been removed, meaning CSI was done with the area, but Nanci's yellow electrical tape remained.

Kitten mused, *I wonder why that old woman hasn't taken that tape.*

This was the first PJ had heard of any "old woman" taking things from the banks of the creek. *Wait, Kitten. What old woman?*

Kitten nodded toward the house with the blue siding and the big screened-in porch. *There's an old woman who lives in that house. Sometimes when we're down here playing, she comes and tries to wash us away with the garden hose.*

PJ and Mutt stared at each other.

PJ said, *Was she here the night all the commotion happened?*

What commotion? Kitten asked.

The night there was a shot and a man fell into the water, and so did I.

Kitten blinked slowly. *I'm not sure I remember any of that. A human fell in the water? Is he okay?*

No, Kitten, he died.

Oh. That's too bad.

I saw that he washed up here, near where that tape is. Do you think the old woman might have seen him?

If she was down here like she usually is, then she must have seen him.

PJ's whiskers were tingling furiously. She washed the sides of her face carefully with her paw. She was almost sure now that there was another witness. Was it too much to think that the old woman Kitten was talking about was out that night? PJ believed in coincidences.

How can we get that woman to come out? PJ asked Kitten.

Kitten's head reared backward at the thought. *You're kidding. I want to avoid her, not bring her out.*

PJ turned to Mutt. *Mutt, bark for me, would you?*

At what?

At that tape. I don't care. At anything.

Mutt sniffed the electrical tape and then started barking at it. Kitten retreated away from them north along the ravine. PJ kept the little cat in sight as she didn't want to lose him again.

It didn't take long. PJ was distracted by keeping Kitten in her view and missed the old woman's approach with the garden hose. Suddenly a spray of water soaked PJ's backside. She howled and ran off after Kitten. Behind her, the woman turned the hose on Mutt, who yelped and ran with PJ. The entire time, the woman was muttering curses that sometimes peaked in a short, staccato yell. PJ recognized those curses and the shape of the dark figure with the hose. It was old Mrs. Norton—Doc Fred's mother.

* * *

From a distance, the animals watched Mrs. Norton hose off the area. The hose didn't quite reach to where the electrical tape was, so she got down on her hands and knees, pulled the tape off, and threw it into the creek. When she was done, there was no sign of any shoe, electrical tape, or crime scene at all. PJ's whiskers were going crazy with tingles at the thought of what all this might mean.

After Mrs. Norton finished and wandered back to the house with the blue siding and large screened-in porch, the animals made their way back toward Stoker Hills. PJ noticed that Kitten would stop every few paces to wash his infected eye with his paw.

Kitten, you need to get that eye looked at.

He looked at PJ from his good eye, doubt clearly evident on his face.

I know a very good veterinarian. She will treat it until it heals.

You're kidding, right? I can't just waltz into a veterinarian's office.

Well, actually you probably could, PJ said, *but you don't have to go alone. I'll take you.*

Kitten looked at her askance. *You? Another cat is going to take me to the vet? What are you going to pay with? Kitty kibble?*

PJ laughed. It was a series of broken snorts and almost sounded like hissing. *No, silly, I'll take you when I'm human.*

Kitten stopped short. All three of the animals stopped then and formed a little circle. Everyone stared at everyone else.

What did you just say? Kitten asked PJ.

I said, I'll take you in the morning when I'm human again.

When you're human again? What does that mean?

Mutt shook his head, his collar jingling amid the noise of cicadas and wood frogs. *She's only a cat part time. During the day she's a human.*

Kitten eyed both Mutt and PJ very closely. Slowly, he said, *The squirrels warned me you were a nut.*

* * *

PJ spent the rest of the night preparing Kitten for his trip to the vet's office. When dawn broke, PJ's body morphed as promised into a short naked woman with long black hair. She quickly went inside her trailer and dressed. Kitten and Mutt followed her inside. She fed them both breakfast and made herself some eggs and bacon. After everyone was well fed, PJ got a cat carrier and coaxed Kitten into it. She had previously prepared Kitten for the experience but still had to grab him by the scruff of the neck and shove him inside.

Kitten howled the entire way to the vet's office. PJ did her best to soothe him, using the few cat language noises she could make as a human, to no avail. By the time they got to the Mayhap Animal Hospital, Kitten was nearly in a frenzy. PJ knew this was going to be a difficult enterprise.

Dr. Noble saw them right away at eight since she had an opening before her surgeries. It took Dr. Noble, PJ, and a vet technician to hold Kitten down so the doctor could diagnose his eye. They gave the screaming Kitten shots for good measure, and while PJ held him, the vet tech glopped a viscous salve into his eye. He wanted to wipe it out with his paw, but PJ wouldn't let him. She held him fast. Dr. Noble wanted to put a cone on Kitten so he couldn't paw at his eye, but PJ knew that would never work. Instead, she took the tube of salve with her and promised to find him daily to give him more until his eye healed.

In the waiting room, PJ ran into Clara. She was wearing all turquoise today. The bright color flattered her red curls and hazel eyes. PJ admired her dangling turquoise earrings greatly.

"Where did you get them?" PJ asked.

"From Lucy, where else?" Lucy ran Lamott's jewelry store and was also a prodigious purveyor of costume jewelry for every taste. Whether you wanted bangles and paste or rarity and gold, Lucy was your go-to.

Clara looked at the clock. She held a cat carrier with a golden-orange cat who had big yellow eyes. "Muffin is due for surgery now," she explained. "He hasn't been eating well, so they're doing an exploratory colonoscopy."

That was more information than PJ wanted to hear. "That's too bad," she said. "I hope it comes back clean."

Clara nodded somberly. "Want to get lunch later? They're still having the 10 percent off special at Lucky Cat."

Lucky Cat Sushi Bar was one of PJ's favorite local restaurants. Aside from the name, the decor appealed greatly to her. It was shades of crimson and vermilion with hundreds of cats displayed on posters, on wallpaper, and on banners. Apparently cats were good luck in Asia, and PJ was only too happy to go along with that.

"Sure. Sounds great. See you at noon among the cats?"

"Perfect."

* * *

They had hardly been seated in a booth near a window before Clara said, "So I heard you went on a date with Jake Tipton. How'd that go? Tell me, tell me!"

PJ was surprised for a moment, then she laughed. "It wasn't a date."

"It wasn't? What was it then? A business lunch?"

"That's not far off, Clara. Apparently he thinks I'm responsible for the Stoker Hills thefts. He wanted to corner me into some kind of confession, I think."

Now it was Clara's turn to be surprised. "You're kidding. You're absolutely kidding."

PJ frowned. "I wish I was. He told me not to leave town."

"Oh, they all say that." Clara waved a hand dismissively. "That jerk. I wondered why he hasn't followed up on the footage you got of them breaking into your trailer."

"He thinks I set that up. To throw suspicion off myself onto someone else, or something like that."

"Oh, PJ, that's silly."

"You're telling me. But the one you should tell is Jake Tipton."

"I think I will. In fact, the next time I see him, I'm going to give him a piece of my mind."

"What does Laura say about the whole thing?"

Clara worked as a librarian and, as such, seemed to have her finger on the pulse of Mayhap. She chatted with everyone who came in and could usually be relied on to have the latest gossip. Beyond that, her sister Laura worked in the municipal building as administrative assistant to the police chief. Both siblings shared the same fondness for gossip, and if Clara didn't know what was happening already from her inquiries, Laura would know.

"Well, like I said, we were wondering why the footage of your trailer break-in wasn't followed up. But I guess it is now. Did you hear they arrested Alex Tate and searched the Tate trailer finally?"

"Did they find anything?"

Clara shrugged. "Some pieces belonging to other people, like watches and stuff like that. But Trent claims he was given those pieces, and there weren't enough to hold him. Detective Tipton thinks there should be much more booty than there was."

"Well, I bet they've been pawning it all. That's why there wasn't that much there."

"Unless it's in your trailer, PJ."

"Very funny."

Clara was laughing. "I know, and you know that you've got a thing for the bling. Better dig out all of your receipts for those shinies you've got hidden around your trailer."

"That's really not funny. Do you think Jake will get a warrant to search my trailer?"

"He hasn't applied for one yet that Laura's told me. But you'll be the first to know if he does."

The waitress came and dropped off drinks and took their orders. PJ sipped her sweet tea. Clara took a long drink of her Coke.

Clara said, "Those two boys are trouble, pure and simple. I wish someone would see that."

"You mean Trent and his friend?"

"Sheldon, yes."

This was the first PJ had heard any name attached to the short boy in the video. "The other one's name is Sheldon?"

"Yes, Sheldon Pike. He lives in Whitesville Township, just across the line. He goes to Mayhap High, though. He's eighteen, so if they could get him for those thefts, he'd be tried as an adult."

PJ knew Trent was only seventeen. "Well, why don't they get off their duffs and get him for those thefts? I caught them red-handed on film. What more do the authorities want?"

"Oh, they always want more. Unless you're unlucky. Then the slightest shred of evidence is enough to send you away for life."

"That's really sad."

"I know. Too bad Trent's not unlucky. Then I'd get more sleep around my place."

"What?"

Clara sucked more Coke through her straw before answering. "That Trent. At least I think it's him. Every night practically, he comes tearing out of Stoker Hills in his mom's ratty old pickup and burns down my street. The thing usually backfires right in front of my house. I always think someone's shooting at the cats. Gives me nightmares."

"Trent goes out on school nights?"

"I'm pretty sure he doesn't care what night it is."

"Where does he go?"

"I have no idea. Probably somewhere nefarious. You know how it is."

PJ's scalp was tingling. She knew that if she had whiskers, she'd have to smooth them down because they'd be feeling so piqued. She felt sure this was a new piece to the puzzle. Could the "shot" everyone heard have been the Tate pickup? If so, why didn't everyone hear it more often? Was it just an unlucky coincidence? PJ didn't think so. She figured she could tell a pickup backfiring from a real gunshot. Or could she? And where was Trent going almost every night? Did it have to do with the thefts?

Two plates of sushi were delivered, and PJ and Clara tucked into the delicacies with enthusiasm. By the time lunch was over, PJ had a good idea of what she would do to investigate the problem of Trent and his nightly excursions.

13

Field Trip

That afternoon, PJ made sure her backup camera was in good working order. When evening came, she transformed in her trailer and waited until deepest twilight to come out. She wanted the cover of darkness, and she hoped she wasn't too late to catch Trent. She needn't have worried. At the Tate trailer, the red pickup was parked under a drooping willow at the edge of the driveway. PJ looked around carefully. Seeing no one, she jumped into the pickup bed. It contained some random debris but was mostly empty. PJ nosed her way under a stained oil cloth and curled up to wait.

The night was calm and filled with the braying of cicadas and the hissing of other insects. Above, thin clouds obscured a waxing moon. PJ heard squirrels chattering nearby and wondered if they were Click and Clack, Kitten's friends. In the distance, Mutt barked. PJ shook her head. That dog was forever breaking free of her trailer and getting his nose into things he shouldn't. PJ had to admit she loved him for that very spunkiness. PJ closed her eyes at the thought, and a quiet purr escaped her.

How long would she have to wait? What was the point of her following Trent, assuming he went out tonight? She mulled these questions over while the last remnants of twilight dissipated in the humid air. She hoped she wouldn't have to wait long. Already her eyes remained closed, and she felt herself pulled into the half-sleep cats enjoyed at a moment's notice. About Trent? Well, PJ wasn't sure why she wanted to see where his nightly trips took him. Call it cat sense; PJ was sure Trent was involved in at least the thefts and possibly Chip's accident too. After all, Mutt had smelled Sheldon Pike's cigarette smoke, and where Sheldon was, there Trent usually was. Thinking such thoughts, PJ slipped into a deeper sleep, nodding off under the warm cloth.

* * *

PJ's eyes flicked wide open. Something had alerted her. She remained very still. She heard the crunching of footsteps on gravel as someone walked toward the pickup. Then, whoever it was opened the front door with a creak and climbed into the driver's seat. The door closed with a loud clunk that made PJ jump. Through the cab window she could see the back of Trent's head.

Showtime, she thought.

Trent started the vehicle and hastily backed up in a circle around the driveway to turn around. PJ slid back and forth in the truck bed with nothing solid to hold on to. This was going to be a wild ride, if the first turn was any indication. Trent drove like a maniac. He sped down the access road and blew through the stop sign at the mouth of Lunar Lane. He gunned it down Lunar Lane, and at the other end, near Clara's house, he slowed briefly to take the turn onto Second Street, then gunned the engine. The pickup backfired loudly, making PJ jump and lose her footing. She sprawled out in the back of the pickup for several moments before she finally regained her balance. She considered jumping out and aborting this ill-advised trip, but curiosity got the better of her as usual, so she hung on. Plus, the truck was speeding, and PJ was worried about possible implications of jumping out of such a fast-moving vehicle. In fact, she was also worried about being thrown from the truck.

After several hair-raising turns, they straightened out on a rural road leading away from Mayhap. Trent was still going much faster than he should, but the ride evened out since they were on steady pavement. PJ took the chance of looking out. She saw cornfields pass and a small lake. She realized they were headed north on Route 421, into the deep countryside. She saw the last few buildings of Mayhap recede into the distance, and then they were in Taft County, speeding along under the moonlight.

PJ hunkered down to wait. She hoped they weren't going far.

About ten minutes later, by PJ's reckoning, Trent slowed and swerved off 421 onto a much smaller road. Less than five minutes after that, he turned onto a gravel road cut between patches of trees. After the trees at the mouth of the road, the area opened up into farmland. Trent drove for several seconds, then pulled up in front of a typical farmhouse and stopped. He opened his door and got out, slamming the door in his wake.

PJ waited until she heard his footsteps diminish, then poked her head over the side of the truck bed. She saw Trent approaching the wrap-around porch of the house. He was carrying a package, large enough that he had to use both hands.

"Yo, old man," Trent called loudly.

PJ ducked her head at the sight of a man coming around the porch's far side. He was carrying a shotgun. PJ's heart raced. She dared to poke her head back out after the initial shock had worn off.

"Hey, Trent," the man with the shotgun said.

Trent nodded at him. The inner door opened, and a man pushed open the screen door.

"'Bout time, boy," a gruff voice said. It belonged to an older man who looked, in PJ's estimation, an awful lot like Trent. The man held the screen door wide, and Trent pushed past him with his package. The man let go of the screen door, and it banged shut, rebounding more than once. PJ realized it hadn't caught on anything; it was simply hanging open. She looked the porch over carefully. The man with the shotgun had returned to wherever he came from.

PJ hunched down and then leaped from the pickup bed. She landed neatly on the gravel beside the truck. She waited. No one came. No one had seen her. Slowly, keeping to dark shadows, she crept to the front porch. The wood was aged and not well taken care of. Without a sound, she ascended to the screen door. She peeped inside. She could hear muffled voices but could see only a few inches past the inner door, which was about six inches open. PJ hooked the screen door with her claws, and pulled it open easily. She took a deep breath and poked her head through the opening made by the heavy inner door.

She saw a living room. It was shabby and unkempt. Newspapers lay in stacks on the coffee table along with numerous plastic beer cups and pizza boxes. The room smelled of rotting food remnants and something chemical that PJ couldn't place. PJ darted inside and raced for the nearest chair.

"Did you see that?" the gruff voice asked.

"What?" Trent said.

Trent and the older man had been standing nearby, on the other side of the heavy front door. PJ had missed them since she was looking the other way when she surveyed the area.

"An animal. A gawd-dang animal. I think it was a raccoon."

"What?"

"You heard me, boy. I think a raccoon just ran in here."

The old man stooped to the ground and looked under the furniture. PJ was squeezed behind the TV stand, praying he didn't find her.

"You're crazy, Pa," Trent said.

From that, PJ gathered the old man was actually Trent's father. That would explain the resemblance.

"C'mon," Trent continued. "I'm tired of carrying this crap. Let's go drop it off in the kitchen."

"Better not be a 'coon in here," the old man said. "Otherwise I'll shoot its tail off and cook it in a stew."

PJ shuddered. Trent and his father left the room, heading down the hall. After a moment, PJ dared to peek out. It looked quiet. She was very, very curious about what was happening in the kitchen. Yet she was also terrified of having her tail shot off and being made into stew. She debated with herself for several seconds before she finally stepped out and crept between the furniture to peer into the hallway. At the other end of the hall stood an open door. The chemical stench was coming from that direction.

PJ pulled back just in time as the two men came out of the kitchen.

"...show you something upstairs," the old man was saying.

In the hall there was a staircase leading up to PJ's left, out of sight. Trent and his father went up the stairs, fortunately not seeing the small black ear listening or yellow eye watching them from the front room. After she heard their steps recede, PJ took the chance of sneaking forward, down the hall, past the steps. Across from the steps was a door, and PJ guessed it probably led to a basement. She wondered briefly what horrible things might be going on down there, but then focused her attention on the kitchen in front of her. She heard cooking sounds and the shuffle of people moving around. She boldly crept up to the door and peeked in.

Two women in what looked like makeshift haz-mat suits were moving around the stove. The chemical stench was coming from whatever was boiling in a large dutch oven. The women wore shower caps, white masks over their noses and mouths, and plastic garments over their regular clothing. One of the woman opened the package Trent had brought. Inside were bottles and various other items that looked like ingredients for whatever noxious stew the women were concocting. On the other side of the kitchen, the back door was open, and PJ could see the shotgun-wielding man standing on the back stoop, smoking.

She decided to try to get a better view for the camera around her neck. She crept into the dimly lit room and kept near to the wall. She braced herself, judged the distance, and jumped to the top of the refrigerator. From there, she got a cat's-eye view of the scene. When she was satisfied she had enough footage of the work these people were doing, she jumped down again. Neither woman responded to the soft thump PJ made when she hit the ground.

PJ peeked around the kitchen door into the hallway. It was clear. Her whiskers tingled, however. Someone had left the basement door open about ten inches. Dare PJ go down into that potential cess pool and have a look? Her need to document the scene overtook her caution, and she crept toward the open door. She didn't hear or see anyone down the wooden steps, but it was dark. Carefully, she stepped onto the stairs and made her way down, her eyes adjusting to the blackness as she went. She knew the camera, with its infrared setting, would have an even better view than she did with her cat vision.

At the base of the stairs, PJ looked up. She screamed. Hanging from the ceiling was a man in shades of blood.

PJ backed away toward the stairs. Her involuntary screech would have everyone running to her, she was afraid. And it would all be for nothing. It wasn't a man hanging from the ceiling; it was only a man's union suit. It must have been a shade of red that looked like blood. Next to it hung T-shirts and jeans, and on other ropes suspended from the ceiling hung sheets and towels. It was only laundry. PJ sniffed the air. The chemical stench that permeated the rest of the house was fainter down here. Instead, she smelled fabric softener and detergent. She had been spooked by the laundry room. She almost laughed at her own stupidity.

Suddenly, the basement was flooded with light.

"Aha! There you are," the old man with the gruff voice said from the top of the stairs.

PJ's eyes were still adjusting to the light. She could hardly see him coming down the stairs toward her.

"See? I told you," the man said to someone over his shoulder. "Only it ain't a 'coon, it's a cat."

PJ backed away as the man came down the stairs.

"Nice kitty," he was crooning. "Let Papa pick you up now."

Of course PJ wasn't about to let this man get ahold of her. He lunged for her and she ran behind the dryer. The man swore a blue streak, then started moving the heavy appliance out so he could reach behind it. PJ jumped out and ran up the stairs. Halfway up she realized the door in front of her was closed. The man was hot on her heels. She was trapped!

She kept running, as if she would smash headlong into the door. At the last second, a miracle happened—the door opened a fraction. She burst through the few inches to freedom and skidded on the tile floor as she turned to race down the hallway. She had a brief image of the short boy, Sheldon Pike, as the one who had opened the door.

"Damn!" Trent's father yelled behind her. "Stop that cat!"

Sheldon pulled out a handgun and shot at PJ. Fortunately, he missed. The bang was so loud that PJ's ears rang for several moments. She hardly heard all the yelling behind her as she raced down the hall and threw herself at the screen door. It opened easily, and she was outside in the blessed night air, flying over the porch and across the driveway where she burrowed into the tall grasses on the other side. She stopped then, fully covered, and peeped between the blades at the scene behind her.

The short boy, Trent's father, and the man with the shotgun had all rallied near the front door. PJ wasn't close enough to hear what they said, but they didn't seem to be chasing her anymore. She felt like the old man was blaming Sheldon for something; whether it was for opening the basement door at the wrong time or shooting his gun in the house, PJ wasn't sure.

After a few moments, the men split up. Trent's father headed back inside. Sheldon lit a cigarette and sat down on a swinging love seat on the front porch. The man with the shotgun went back around the house, presumably to watch the rear entrance.

PJ breathed many sighs of relief. She had gotten in, gotten decent footage of wrongdoing, and gotten out in one piece. She smiled to herself. It was only then she realized that Trent's red pickup was gone. Her ride home had disappeared.

14

Interrogated

It took PJ all night to return home, partly because she kept getting distracted by fox holes and field mice. By the time she came to Main Street, streaks of pink lit the eastern sky. She transformed in the alley behind Bones Pizzeria and quickly dressed in her emergency black shorts and shirt. She stretched the small cat-pack across her shoulders, left the collar around her neck, and headed for Lunar Lane.

When PJ rounded her driveway, she saw Jake's marked SUV. She didn't see Jake. Henry was in the back, though, watching her as she approached. She waggled her ears when she passed the vehicle, and Henry barked at her. At the sound, Jake came out from behind her trailer.

"Oh, there you are, PJ," he said.

"What's up, Jake?"

He frowned. "I need you to come talk to me."

"Well, come inside. Just let me change and start a pot of coffee."

"No, I really think we need to talk at the station."

Panic flooded PJ. "Are you arresting me?"

"Please don't make this harder than it needs to be."

PJ looked around. No one else seemed to be up this early. But where was Robert? His secretary sat next to a police scanner and usually got all the juice. PJ would have expected if Jake was officially here to arrest her, Robert would have heard.

"Can I at least change? I'm a little chilly."

He looked her up and down. She shifted her weight between her bare feet and rubbed her arms. Her throat was suddenly so dry she could hardly swallow.

"You're fine. Please step over to the vehicle."

He held an arm out and indicated the SUV. Something in PJ cracked at his commanding voice. Cold adrenaline flooded her, and she saw only the gun at Jake's waist and the silver of his tie clip.

"Ms. Taylor? Now, please."

Reason failed PJ and she bolted. She ran behind her trailer and thrashed through the woods. Her breath was hot in the morning air, and she sweated like crazy. She felt dizzy and more than a little confused. Behind her, she heard yelling, then barking. Deep from her addled mind a thought came— she wouldn't get away. She was making this all worse. She had to stop.

All of that had gotten her about thirty yards from the trailer. Reason prevailed at last and she stopped. She turned. Henry ran at her, teeth bared, barking and growling.

She screamed.

A second before Henry jumped on her, a huge black mass flew in from the side and knocked him from his path. Mutt. PJ's first thought was intense gratitude, but as the dogs wrestled, she quickly became freaked out instead.

"No! Jake, heel him! Stop, Mutt!"

Jake ran down the ravine toward the struggling dogs, hand on his weapon. Mutt was significantly larger than Henry and mad as hell. But Henry was lither and faster, extremely well trained, and dressed in a bullet-proof vest, making him nearly impregnable. What happened next seemed to be in slow motion.

Henry threw Mutt off of him.

Jake had his gun out and took aim.

"No!"

Without thinking, PJ jumped between Jake and Mutt.

Jake's eyes widened. His trigger finger jerked. The gun flashed. PJ screamed again. She was right there, nearly point-blank, but Jake's aim was off. It took PJ a moment to figure out why.

A furry black animal had Jake's pant leg in its teeth and was wildly pulling on it, unbalancing the hapless detective. From out of nowhere, two squirrels had jumped on Jake's arm. One was on his shoulder, claws out, while the other dangled by its teeth from Jake's elbow.

"Shit!" Jake yelled. "Get them off me!"

PJ couldn't believe it. Kitten and his two squirrel friends had nearly felled Detective Tipton. She stared, open-mouthed, for several seconds as Jake stumbled around, animals flying. Henry had returned to his master and was barking and barking. Mutt was making a kind of wheezing whine, which PJ recognized as laughter.

Jake waved his arm and leg. His gun hand flailed. Henry barked. The squirrels and Kitten held fast.

"PJ, get them off me! Help!"

PJ made a low growl in her throat to activate her camera. This was the craziest sight she had ever seen.

"Don't just stand there," Jake yelled. "Help me!"

PJ shrugged and held her hands out. "What am I supposed to do?"

"I don't care! Something! And do it quick!"

PJ ran back to her trailer and grabbed her garden hose. She unraveled it as far as it would go and ran back to where Jake was still struggling with the animals. She sprayed Jake, soaking him. It worked—the squirrels scampered away, and Kitten let go and ran. PJ kinked the hose to stop the flow and eyed Jake, who stood dripping before her, his gun held limply at his side. The look on his face was indescribable, a mix of pure rage and horrified chagrin. And PJ knew she had it all on video.

* * *

Half an hour later, PJ sat in a small, nondescript room in the municipal building. Its only contents were a wooden table and a small stack of chairs, two of which were out for use. The blinds were drawn, and the light overhead was anemic and fluorescent. The only sound was the faint buzzing of that light, save for every few minutes when someone might walk by the door and a murmured conversation would interrupt the hypnotic buzzing. There was a window in the door with blinds on the outside, so whoever wanted to could see in should they desire. Other than that, the room was four green walls and a yellow linoleum floor. PJ shivered. She had a warm cup of coffee in front of her, but her bare feet on the linoleum made her particularly aware of her skimpy apparel. She wished she had on boots and a fluffy sweater. She passed the time filling her mind with thoughts of warm things, such as fire pits and space heaters. She kept crossing and recrossing her legs in an effort to keep moving and keep warm. Her arms were firmly crossed over her chest. She sighed.

She didn't know how much time had passed before Jake finally showed up, having changed into jeans and a lumberjack's shirt. She envied him his boots and warm clothing. He came into the room carrying a fat file, carefully closed the door, and sat down at the table opposite her. She stared at him silently, waiting for the inevitable.

"You should know everything in here is recorded," Jake said. He indicated a black semi-sphere on the ceiling. A red light glowed in its depth.

PJ said nothing.

Jake cleared his throat. He smiled at PJ. "We didn't get off to a very good start this morning."

She couldn't help it—she smiled back. "Sorry about that. I don't know what got into me, or into those animals. Are you all right?"

He nodded. "I'll live. But I do have some questions for you, PJ. Are you ready to answer them?"

"I just want to get this over with and get home. I'm freezing."

"Oh, do you want me to get you a blanket or something?"

"Gosh, Jake, that would be great. Could you please?"

He got up and retreated from the room, taking his file folder with him. PJ froze for several more minutes before he returned with a uniformed female officer carrying a blanket. She handed it to PJ and then left the room without saying anything. Jake sat opposite PJ again while she wrapped the stiff emergency blanket around herself. She immediately started to feel a little better.

"Thanks," she said.

"Of course," Jake said. "Sorry it took me so long. I had to get changed, as you know. My suit was soaking wet."

PJ blushed. "Sorry about that."

He chuckled. "I suppose I can see the humor in it, now that it's over."

"You did look pretty funny with two squirrels hanging off your arm."

"Don't forget about the cat biting my leg."

PJ snorted. "Yeah."

"All right, PJ. Well I'll ask you a few questions, and you answer them to the best of your ability, okay?"

PJ took a sip of her tepid coffee. "Sure. Fire away."

"Where were you the nights of February 12 and 16?"

PJ stared at him. "I don't know. Is there anything special about them?"

"Two days before Valentine's Day and two days after."

Valentine's Day hadn't been special for PJ. Since she was single, it was just another day.

"Sorry, I have no idea. Probably at home in my trailer?"

"Is there anyone who can vouch for your whereabouts?"

"Mutt?"

"PJ, you're not making this easy."

She stared into the coffee mug. "I'm trying. I honestly don't know where I was. Most nights I am simply at home, watching TV or on my computer. That's probably where I was."

He wrote something down on a pad of paper "All right, PJ. How about the night of March 21?"

PJ had to think for a bit. "You mean, Saturday two weeks ago?"

Jake nodded. It was the night of Chip Greene's unfortunate trip down the swollen waters of the ravine.

"A dam broke that night, apparently. The ravine behind my home was filled with raging water."

Jake nodded again. "Where were you? At home?"

PJ took a deep breath. Now she had to remember everything she'd told Robert and recount it for Jake. She hoped she could keep it all straight.

"Well," she began, "I had been going out at night for a little while, trying to acclimate to it."

"Okay, stop," Jake said. "Why do you need to acclimate to the night?"

PJ sighed. "I have an extreme phobia of night. It's not just darkness, it's the actual night. Usually I stay in my trailer with all the lights on. I can only sleep in the light."

"All right. Continue please."

PJ swallowed. "Well, that night at around midnight, I was out for a little bit wearing my light goggles."

"Explain what those are."

"They're goggles, but with lights around the rims. I'm thinking some of my phobia might be physiological, so if my eye area is filled with light, perhaps I can be outside at night and it won't be as bad."

"So even though you know it is night and you're outside, if you have a lot of light around your eye area, you're okay?"

"Well, not really. But I can at least be outside. I'm working on it."

"All right. Did you see anything when you were outside?"

"Well..." PJ shifted her weight around inside the blanket. Jake looked at her expectantly. "I saw Chip Greene and Alex Tate down by Chip's trailer."

Jake wrote on his pad. "So you saw Chip Greene and Alex Tate. What were they doing?"

"Nothing. Standing by the side of the water and talking. I couldn't see that well, but I heard Alex bleating."

"Bleating?"

"Well, you know. He's autistic. Sometimes he makes a sound like a goat. I call it bleating."

Jake nodded, still writing on his paper.

"Anyway, I turned away for a second, and then I think I saw Chip fall in the water."

Jake stopped writing and stared at her. "You saw Chip fall in? By himself? What was Alex doing?"

"Well, when I looked up again, Alex was trying to rescue Chip."

"You saw that? I thought you could hardly see anything."

PJ rubbed her eyes. "I shifted the goggles to my forehead so I could see a little better. And I saw Alex trying to pull Chip from the water. But then Alex fell in too."

Jake frowned. "Okay, so now both of them are in the water. Then what happened."

"Well, uh, Alex was floundering around trying to swim. And I didn't see what happened to Chip. He had disappeared."

"You didn't go over to try to help them?"

"I was quite a ways away."

"Still. I would have thought you would want to help them, or at least go call the authorities to help them."

PJ sighed. "I was terrified. By the night, and by what I saw. I started to go over to them but I stumbled and fell in the river myself."

Jake's eyebrows rose. "You fell in the water too?"

"Yes. And I hit my head when I did."

"You could have been killed."

PJ wondered if she should tell Jake about seeing Chip lying on the side of the water near old Mrs. Norton's house. She decided to focus on answering Jake's questions and not offer any additional commentary. She realized she was probably walking a thin line with him.

Jake checked his notes and flipped through his file for several moments. Then he raised his head and looked at PJ.

"So you hit your head right after you fell in the water?"

"Uh, well, no."

"No?"

"I slid to the south, down the river for a little while first. It was deep. I couldn't get my footing. The water carried me along fast."

"That must have been terrifying."

"You have no idea. I was sure I was going to die. And I lost my goggles and my robe. So I was naked in the freezing cold water."

Jake shook his head. "I'm sorry about that. But, please continue. You were carried downstream for a ways?"

"Yes. And, well, I thought I saw Chip lying on the side of the water."

"What?"

"By old Mrs. Norton's house. I could have sworn I caught a glimpse of him there, lying on the bank."

Jake didn't say anything. Instead, he wrote furiously.

"But then I hit my head on a rock, and that's it, that's all I remember. Just a glimpse, then boom—out."

Jake was still writing with most of his attention. "Hm," he said absently.

"Can I go now?" PJ asked.

Jake looked up at her, his pen paused over the page. "What?"

"That's all I remember. When can I go home?"

"Are you uncomfortable?"

"I'm okay." In actuality, PJ was feeling more than a little nervous, but since she had the blanket, she wasn't feeling so bad physically anymore.

"I'm afraid we'll have to go over this a few more times until I really have it straight."

PJ sighed.

* * *

PJ felt like hours had passed when a knock came on the door. Jake got up and went to the door, leaving PJ with nothing but her blanket and the dregs of cold coffee in her mug.

On the other side of the closed door, she thought she heard a familiar voice. She strained to listen but could only hear mumbling. The mumbling went on for quite some time. At points, the voices were raised almost enough for PJ to make out some words.

"...sister," she heard Jake say. She couldn't hear the response, but after hearing that word, she recognized Robert's baritone voice.

After some more negotiation, the door opened and Robert entered with Jake. Robert took one of the chairs from the stack and set it up at the end of the table so he was cater-corner from both PJ and Jake. Jake sat back down. His face was flushed, and he didn't look happy. The three of them sat there and looked at each other for several moments.

"Sorry I couldn't get here sooner, PJ," Robert said.

Before PJ could say anything, Jake said, "Robert is here out of professional courtesy. I'm running the show, though, make no mistake." He glared at PJ.

Up until then, PJ had thought it was going fairly well. She really thought Jake had believed her about everything. When he said that and gave her his angry look, PJ suddenly wondered if she was in more trouble than she had thought. Robert didn't look happy. PJ swallowed heavily but said nothing.

"All right, PJ," Jake said, "How about now that your brother's here, you start telling the truth?"

"What?" PJ's mouth dropped open.

"Your statement. It seems highly implausible."

"What do you mean? What part?"

"All of it."

"What are you saying?" PJ started to shake under the blanket.

"I'm saying you were never there that night."

"What?"

"You were never there, and you never saw Chip Greene or Alex Tate."

"Yes, I did—I told you. It all happened just like I said."

Jake sighed. "PJ, you're a very good liar. We all know that."

PJ looked at Robert. Robert was staring at the tabletop and said nothing. PJ looked at Jake. Jake stared intently back.

"I don't know what to say to that," she said.

"How about the truth?"

"That is the truth. What you've been writing down. That's the truth."

"PJ, honestly. You expect me to believe you happened to be out at exactly the time Alex Tate pushed Chip Greene into the water—"

"He didn't push him. Chip fell."

"So you say. You expect me to believe you could see that with your face full of light on a dark moonless night?"

"Well, I saw shadows. I could tell who they were because I know them."

"Right. And then you stumbled and fell into the water before you could help or call 911."

"Yes."

"That's bull and you know it."

"Robert, why is he saying this?" PJ asked her brother. Robert remained silent. He lifted his wrist and looked at his watch.

"PJ, you like to be where the action is, right?"

"Uh, what does that mean?"

"I mean, you like to be the center of attention. You usually are, with your photos and videos of anything important that happens in town, right?"

"Well, I'm not sure—"

"So you figured, Chip Greene's drowning was the biggest event of a lifetime, and you wanted to be involved. You cobbled together a nice little story that covered the evidence as you saw it. And you came up with this cock-and-bull about light goggles and a trip through the river."

"No. No, that's not what happened. I want a lawyer."

"You're not under arrest, PJ. Should you be?"

Cold fear flooded PJ. "No. No, of course not."

"Then why don't you admit you made it all up?"

"I didn't. You know, a girl found me the next morning. Ask her."

"Ah yes, your niece's friend, Bridget. A girl detective with an overactive imagination. She says she found you naked and washed up on the bank near her house."

"She did find me there. I had hit my head. I was out all night."

"We didn't find any evidence of anyone washing up near the girl's house. And, PJ, where did your goggles and robe go? They haven't washed up anywhere either."

That was definitely a hole in PJ's story. She hadn't tried to plant a robe or goggles anywhere because she was afraid she'd get it wrong and just make things worse. Plus, they could plausibly have disappeared in the raging river, right?

"I don't know why they haven't," PJ said. "I'm sure if you keep looking, they'll turn up."

"You mean when you plant them, right?"

PJ shut her mouth into a tight line. She wondered if she should keep quiet now and refuse to say anything. She'd already said a lot. All there was to say, in fact.

"I'm not answering any more questions."

"Oh, come on, PJ. You don't fool me."

"This is ridiculous."

PJ looked at Robert. Robert was scratching his chin. He looked at his watch again.

"I told my brother what happened," PJ said. "Why don't you ask him?"

"Ask your brother? Do you think I'm stupid? Of course he'll say whatever you told him to say."

Robert rolled his eyes but continued to say nothing.

"That's not fair," PJ said. "He wouldn't lie for me."

"I think—" Jake didn't get past those words before there was a knock and the door opened. PJ saw Vicky and with her was Liam Pfefferheim. Liam walked into the room. He was in a slick dark suit with a pastel blue tie and carried a briefcase.

"The interrogation is over, Detective," Liam said. "I'm taking PJ home."

15

Video

Robert's office was three rooms above a bank in the lot of a mini-mall on Jupiter Street, Mayhap's main road to I-65. Entrance to his domain was from the back, through a nondescript door that read "Federal Bureau of Investigation, Mayhap Field Office, head Robert Taylor." Robert had one full-time staff, a cheery woman named Jolene with blond hair and a generous frame. Jolene carried out most administration for Robert. Other than that, he used the facilities and personnel of Sheriff Denning or the local police department whenever he needed CSI or manpower.

When PJ parked in the lot the morning after her interrogation, she saw Robert standing in the window of his office overlooking Jupiter Street. She got out of her car and waved, and he waved back. Then he flipped the blinds closed, concealing himself. Upstairs, Jolene opened the door before PJ reached it.

"Hey, lady," Jolene said.

They hugged briefly. PJ liked Jolene a lot. She was a smartie with a tinge of red in her hair, bright blue eyes, and gold, thin-rimmed glasses. She was much taller than PJ, very womanly and matronly, PJ always thought. She was indeed like a mother figure to PJ and very protective of her employer's baby sister. Today Jolene was in a flowery blouse, navy slacks, black shoes, and dangly gold earrings, which PJ immediately complimented her on.

"Thanks! The man is back there waiting for you."

PJ thanked her, walked to Robert's half-open door, and knocked softly.

"Come on in, PJ," he said.

PJ closed the door, and they sat facing each other in the two chairs in front of his big desk.

"What's up?" Robert asked.

"I have something for you," PJ said. She pulled a thumb drive from her pocket and handed it to Robert.

He turned it over in his hands. "What's this? Did you finally get footage of the Greene-Tate confrontation?"

"I wish. No, this is even better." PJ beamed at her brother.

He stood and went around his desk to plug the drive into his computer. After scanning it for viruses or other intrusive problems, he opened the single file on it. It was video PJ had taken in Trent's father's house. PJ came around the desk and watched over Robert's shoulder. First, Trent got out of the truck and walked to the front door where his father greeted him. Then the footage cut to inside, where PJ had filmed the women in the kitchen opening the package and cooking their contraband stew. Finally, there was brief footage of the short boy firing his gun. The scene was from a weird angle and cut out suddenly, but PJ included it because she felt it was crucial to any case against Sheldon Pike.

Robert watched the footage in silence. He clicked the file closed and rubbed his chin.

"Well?" PJ asked. "What do you think?"

Robert stood abruptly, nearly knocking PJ backward. "PJ," he began, then stopped. He rounded his desk and paced back and forth in front of it. PJ watched him, becoming more and more aware that Robert was really upset about something.

"What's wrong?" she said. "Isn't it obvious what's happening? Isn't this your domain?"

Robert ran his fingers through his hair. "You have no idea what you've done, PJ."

"What? What does that mean?"

"Who else has seen this footage?"

PJ swallowed. "Uh. Well, I sent a copy to Sheriff Denning's office."

"Oh no." Robert stopped pacing briefly to stare at PJ. "Please tell me you didn't."

"Actually, I did."

Robert waved his arms at PJ angrily. "You should always consult me first with something like this. I can't believe it. You've blown the whole thing now."

"What? Blown what?" PJ was completely taken aback by Robert's response. Instead of congratulating her on a case well solved, he was acting as if she were the bad guy.

"PJ, you—"

"I what?"

Robert glared at her. Further conversation was stopped, however, by Jolene knocking briefly, opening the door, and poking her head around the jamb.

"Franklin's here," she said.

"Of course he is," Robert said. "It's the worst timing. Darn it, PJ."

PJ was starting to feel hurt and more than a little offended by Robert's reaction. "Who's Franklin?" she said.

Robert came around the desk again and turned off his monitor. He sat in his desk chair and motioned PJ to sit down in one of the chairs in front of his desk. "Fine. Show him in, Jolene."

Jolene said, "Special Agent Andy Franklin," and opened the door wide to admit a husky man in his mid-forties. PJ sized him up. Whereas her brother was tall, a hair over six feet, Franklin was much shorter—she would have put him at five-seven or so. Both men were fit and muscular, but Robert had more of a triathlete's build whereas Franklin was clearly a former body-builder, stocky and barrel-chested. Robert was in a charcoal suit with a silver tie; Franklin wore a navy suit with a maroon tie. Robert's hair was still dark brown and luxurious, whereas Franklin's hair consisted of gray and white bristles cropped short into a military-style crew cut. Franklin had light brown eyes in a similar shade to Robert's, but without the golden flecks sparkling throughout.

The three of them exchanged handshakes. Meeting Franklin, PJ felt her hackles rise. She had wanted to talk to Robert alone, of course, and grill him about his odd reaction to the video. Also, she wondered why another G-man was here. Was Franklin going to be Robert's new partner or something? PJ hoped not. Robert seemed to work best alone, and to be honest, she didn't want to share him. She was like an unofficial partner, she realized, and if Franklin was to be more permanent, her role would be in question.

"PJ," Franklin repeated, after Robert introduced her. "You have amazing eyes. They seem to be yellow in the light."

PJ wasn't sure that was a compliment. "Uh, thanks."

Franklin smiled. "I've heard of you. Your reputation precedes you."

"I hope that's a good thing."

Franklin sat in the chair opposite PJ in front of the desk. He folded his hands together in his lap. "So what do you think of the Greene-Tate business, PJ?"

PJ's eyes widened. Franklin was apparently the type to get right down to business without any small talk. She glanced at Robert. His face showed nothing. He was rubbing his chin and looking nowhere in particular.

PJ refocused on Franklin. "I think it's horrible. I think it was an accident and Alex Tate is being railroaded."

Franklin nodded. "Seems like that's what your brother here thinks too."

"What do you think?" PJ asked.

Andy fidgeted with his fingers. "I think it's hard to say. We weren't there that night, were we?"

The way he looked at PJ when he said that sent a chill streaking down her spine. The chill turned into an icy coldness at his next words.

"Pardon me, you were there, weren't you?"

PJ had a sudden flashback to being interrogated by Jake and couldn't help herself from saying, "I was?"

Franklin smiled. "I read that you washed up south of where Chip Greene went into the ravine waters. It was in Robert's report."

This was the first PJ had heard of any report that Robert had made. But, in retrospect, it was obvious. He was FBI. They reported everything. In fact, Franklin was probably composing his report of their conversation in his head as they spoke.

"I slipped and fell into the water," PJ said.

Franklin's face was implacable. "Is it a common occurrence for you to turn up naked around the neighborhood in the morning? Common enough for you to forget it?"

PJ's mouth dropped open. Now she thought she knew where this was going. Special Agent Andy Franklin was another Detective Jake Tipton. This was another interrogation. Now she had to be extra careful, because in the grand scheme of law enforcement, this Franklin man was at least as rarefied as Robert. Not like Jake, a small-town cop whose word had to be balanced against the big, bad FBI brother. No, Franklin was infinitely more dangerous. PJ swallowed.

Before PJ could say anything, Robert spoke up. "Andy, is that why you came all this way? To interrogate my sister?"

Franklin smoothed his bristly hair with a hand. "Sorry, Robert. That came out wrong."

PJ wondered how it could have come out right.

Franklin tapped his head with a finger. "Sorry, PJ. You know us agents. Always curious, always asking stupid questions."

PJ felt her face redden. "I can't help what happened."

Franklin seemed determined to change tack. "Did you hear the prime suspect is back home?"

"Who?" PJ said.

"Alex Tate."

"He's back home? That's great. So the judge let him go?"

"His mom posted bail. But I don't think the judge was impressed with the case because bail was awfully low. Twenty dollars."

"Wow. Is that usual?"

"It is if the judge wants to send a message to the DA to seriously reconsider his case."

PJ couldn't help sitting up extra straight and smiling. "That's awesome. I knew Alex was innocent."

"How?"

PJ's shoulders drooped again. "What?"

"You saw something that made you think the Tate boy was innocent?"

PJ looked at Robert. He was studying his hands, which rested on his desk at the moment.

"I'm sure it was in Robert's report," PJ said.

"I'd love to hear it from you, PJ," Franklin said.

PJ crossed her arms. "I didn't see that much. But from what I did see, Alex fell in the water himself, trying to help Chip get out."

"And Alex was rescued by a big dog, apparently. Is that right?"

"Mutt."

"Mutt?"

"The big dog who rescued Alex. He's a Saint Bernard mix."

"Is he yours?"

"As much as you can say anyone 'owns' an animal, I guess."

"Oh, right. I guess we can never really own another sentient creature."

PJ felt herself warm significantly to Franklin when he said that. At least the man had his priorities straight when it came to animal rights.

"What else did you see?" Franklin said.

"Not much. I fell into the water and hit my head. I might have caught a glimpse of Chip on the bank downstream. But it's all fuzzy."

"Anything else?"

"No."

"From what I've been hearing at HQ, you seem to be close to almost everything interesting that happens in Mayhap, PJ."

PJ's eyes narrowed. "What does that mean?"

"It's just that you seem to either have knowledge of prime events or actual photographic footage of them. You don't happen to have any pictures of the Greene-Tate incident, do you? Like maybe some footage you're keeping to yourself because you don't think it means anything? Or because it doesn't seem to mean what you want it to?"

PJ's scalp crawled. It was almost as if Franklin knew she did have some scant footage of the event, which she had decided to withhold because it could have been used against Alex as much as for him. She stared Franklin in the eyes and said, "Nope. Not this time. I know I'm known as a terrible busybody, but this time my sources failed me."

"Your sources?"

"I'm not the one who takes all those photos and video, at least not all the time. Some of it gets anonymously sent to my inbox."

"Oh. I see."

"You know what 'PJ' stands for, right?"

"Tell me," Franklin said.

"Peeping Jane."

Franklin laughed.

"It's a nickname I've had since I was about ten." PJ looked at Robert. "Which incident was it? The flying turkey one?"

Robert chuckled. "No, I think it was the one about the haystack."

Franklin's eyes twinkled. "Now you have to explain what those are."

"Well," PJ said, "the flying turkey one was when someone was breaking into the Amish barns and stealing turkeys. Turns out it was a guy running a dog-fighting ring, trying to get free food. He thought their religion prevented them from going to the police."

Franklin laughed. "Aren't you glad they're stupid?"

PJ chuckled. "Sometimes we're stupid, so I guess it's good the bad guys usually are too."

Franklin and Robert nodded in unison.

Robert said, "The haystack incident was darker. A girl was attacked in a barn, and the main suspect denied it. Poor girl. Then PJ let it be known we thought there were probably traces of clues in the haystacks, and we caught him red-handed searching for them."

Franklin guffawed. "That's amazing. You got a perp looking for the proverbial needle in a haystack—literally."

"Yep," PJ said.

Robert winked at her. "She's good, Andy. Real good. Good for this community."

PJ smiled at her brother. She was surprised at his warm endorsement of her. She hoped she wasn't getting him into any trouble by backing her.

Franklin said, "I can see that. She's got a brain on her. Unlike her brother."

"Ha, ha." Robert said sarcastically.

PJ chortled. "I think the brains in our family run on the X chromosomes, so he only got half of them."

All three of them laughed uproariously.

* * *

After work, Robert headed for PJ's. By the time he got there, the sun had set, and PJ was nowhere to be found.

"PJ?" he called, looking through her trailer. There was no sign of her.

He came back outside onto the stoop and contemplated where PJ might be. He saw a small black tabby cat with a jeweled collar watching him from the driveway.

"Hello there," he said.

The tabby closed her eyes at him, then opened them again.

"Don't suppose you know where the woman who lives here is?"

The cat was silent.

Robert ran his hand through his hair. "I guess not."

He needed to talk to PJ. After she had left, Franklin had given him a thorough grilling about her role in the Greene-Tate case. Apparently, Franklin was more on the side of Jake Tipton and inclined to believe PJ made up her story to get attention.

Robert also had other pressing issues to talk to PJ about. But he guessed they would have to wait until morning. He wasn't about to wander into the woods around her trailer and look for her. He supposed she was out with those darn light goggles she'd been trying. Who knew when she'd be back?

He got back in his sedan and started it. As he pulled away, he saw the tabby cat watching him from the stoop. Her eyes struck an unconscious chord in Robert, and he wondered why he found the cat so compelling. He didn't stop to think about it much, instead being preoccupied with all the other things on his mind.

16

Nanci

The next morning, PJ sat inside Coffee on Main and nursed a mug of hot chocolate. She had a copy of the *Mayhap Mirror* and was reading the crime beat. She was irked to see Sam Collins had beat her to the punch. The police had raided Trent's father's house, arresting four and picking up nearly two pounds of crystal meth for their trouble. PJ was happy the house was out of business but annoyed she hadn't been the one to publicly break the story. She knew she'd been neglecting her freelance duties in all the confusion surrounding the Greene-Tate business.

Robert pushed open the double doors and walked toward PJ's booth. He was in a navy suit with a gold tie that set off the highlights in his eyes. Those eyes were flashing emotions at PJ, and not good ones. PJ wondered if Robert was more angry or chagrined.

"What's wrong?" she asked as he sat down.

He pointed to the paper lying next to her. "I take it you saw the bust."

"Yeah. But isn't that a good thing?"

The waitress came by, and Robert ordered coffee and an omelet. PJ ordered eggs Benedict with a side of toast and bacon.

After the waitress left them alone, Robert stared at PJ, his lips pressed into a thin line.

"What aren't you telling me?" PJ said.

Robert was silent. Before PJ could grill him further, the waitress dropped off Robert's coffee. He took it up and sipped from it.

"No really, Robert," PJ tried again. "What's wrong with the bust? Why are you upset about it?"

"You know I can't talk about open and active cases."

"Oh. So the investigation is still ongoing?"

"Yes."

"I read they arrested two women and two men. Was Sheldon Pike among those they arrested?"

"I'm not at liberty to say."

"You know, he was there the night Chip Greene went in the water."

"What?!"

"He smokes these distinct cigarettes, and I smelled them."

"And your story changes again. PJ, you've got to drop the whole Greene-Tate thing. Let the system do its job. You know they released Tate. Isn't that what you wanted?"

"Well, they released him for now. But he won't get far if Detective Tipton is still gunning for him."

"How do you know Detective Tipton isn't gunning for you?"

"He thinks I made everything up, that I wasn't involved at all. So I guess he's not going to try to pin anything on me for that."

"And what about the thefts at Stoker Hills?"

"That was Trent and Sheldon Pike. They should be in jail. Why won't you talk to me about Sheldon Pike?"

Robert sighed. "PJ, let's change the subject. There's something I have to talk to you about."

"Okay, fine. But there's something I wanted to talk to you about also."

"All right, you first."

"Who is Special Agent Franklin? Why is he here? Is he going to be your new partner or something?"

Robert laughed. "No, he's not going to be my partner. He'll be the opposite, really."

"What does that mean?"

Robert took a swig of his coffee. "He's here to investigate me. He'll be doing my annual performance report."

"What? Investigate you? That doesn't sound good."

"It's routine, actually. Every year our performance is analyzed. You know, next week I have to take a polygraph."

"What!? A lie detector test? Why?"

"PJ, I thought I told you that before. It is standard every year in the Bureau. They have to make sure I haven't gone over to the dark side."

PJ ran her fingers through her hair. "That sounds stressful."

"It is."

"What does Franklin have to do with it? Is he giving the polygraph?"

"No, I'll drive down to HQ in Indy for the polygraph. Andy was just here to question me about my recent reports."

"Your recent reports. . . you mean about the Greene-Tate business?"

"Yes. And the Stoker Hills thefts. Both of the reports featured you, PJ. And Franklin got the idea from somewhere that not only are you a busybody, but you make up events when you're not involved."

"By 'somewhere,' you mean he got that idea from Jake Tipton."

"That's who I would have guessed as well. I'm thinking the bastard is trying to go over my head to get me in trouble. I imagine he brought up the fact that you're my sister so my judgment may be faulty where you're concerned."

"That's bull."

"I know that and you know that, PJ. Just because you're my sister doesn't mean you get a free pass. If you break the law in any way, I'll bring you in myself."

"I know that. I'm not a criminal; I love the law. I uphold it as much as you do."

Robert nodded.

"So is Franklin going to make trouble for you? Give you a bad report?"

"I'm not sure. He seemed congenial by the time he left yesterday. And I think he was positively impressed by you. But it's hard to say. He might just be lulling us into a false sense of security."

"Great."

"But, PJ, that's not what I wanted to talk to you about."

"Okay, so talk. What's up?"

Robert became quiet all of a sudden. He took a swig of his coffee and ran his hand through his hair. In spite of declaring he wanted to talk, he said nothing for several moments.

PJ stared at him. She could swear he looked nervous. "Robert, are you all right? What's wrong?"

His brow furrowed. He opened his mouth but nothing came out. He shut his mouth again.

"Did something happen? Am I in trouble?"

He eyed PJ. "For once, this isn't about you, PJ. At least, not directly." Robert looked around. There wasn't anyone sitting close to them, and no one seemed interested in their conversation. Still, he lowered his voice so PJ could hardly hear it. "It's about Nanci."

PJ's hackles rose immediately. "Nanci? What about her?"

"Shh."

PJ lowered her voice as well. "Now I'm worried. Is she okay?"

"She's all right. I think."

PJ felt the blood drain from her face. "You think? What's happened, Robert? What's wrong with her? Was she caught trespassing?"

Robert frowned. "What makes you think that?"

"Her little investigation club. Isn't that what she's been doing?"

"Oh, that. No one's complained about that as far as I've heard. She just walks up and down the ravine with Bridget, looking for clues with her magnifying glass. It's cute, really."

"Then what? Spit it out, dude. You're freaking me out here."

Robert sipped his coffee. He ran a hand through his hair again. His hair was already sticking up from his previous intrusion and now looked positively spiky.

"Robert, what?"

"It's hard for me to talk about this. We haven't mentioned it in years. And I never wanted to believe it."

PJ's heart thudded against her rib cage. "Spit it out! Are you trying to give me a heart attack? What's wrong with Nanci?"

Robert opened his mouth, but no words came out. He shut his mouth again. He smoothed his tie against his chest.

"Goodness, Robert. Whatever it is, we'll deal with it. Now tell me so I can help. What's she done? Is she in trouble at school?"

"No, not that I know of. She always does really well."

Suddenly, PJ had a thought. Nanci was twelve. It was possible her time of change was nigh. "Is it puberty?"

Robert froze and stared at PJ. "Puberty?"

"You know. Her... woman's... thing."

"Oh. You mean her period."

PJ blushed.

"Jeepers, PJ. Don't be embarrassed about that. I'm not. But it's not actually anything like that. I don't think, anyway."

PJ sighed. "I'm out of ideas then. You're going to have to tell me."

"PJ," Robert began. "Nanci, uh..."

"Yes?"

"Well, it's stupid." Robert snickered at himself.

"Fine, so tell me anyway."

Robert took a deep breath and looked PJ directly in the eyes. "PJ, Nanci thinks she's been turning into a cat at night."

17

Camping

That Friday, PJ and Robert were in Robert's pickup headed to school to pick up Nanci. After Robert's incredible revelation, PJ could only think that they needed some time together, the three of them, alone, where she could watch Nanci and see if Robert's fears were actualized. They decided to go on a campout, just the three of them. Didi was happy to have a weekend to herself.

Robert pulled into the middle school parking lot and stopped. They were a few minutes early.

Robert rubbed his chin. "It's impossible, right, PJ?" he said. "People don't turn into cats."

For nearly two decades, they hadn't talked about what Robert had seen that night in the weeks after their mom's death when PJ moved in with him. They had avoided talking about the issue for so long that PJ found herself unable to speak for several moments.

"I need your help with this, PJ," Robert said. "This is far outside my expertise, if you can call it that. I can't believe it. But she's my daughter. My baby. I can't turn my back on her."

"You mean like you turned your back on me."

Suddenly, there were tears in Robert's eyes. He swallowed and the waters lessened, but the sheen stayed in his golden-brown eyes. "That's not fair, PJ. I did the best I could with you."

PJ dropped her gaze to his brown-booted feet. "I'm sorry. That was mean. You have done a lot for me—more than I probably deserve."

"PJ, I'm sorry, but this isn't about you. Or maybe it is. But not in that way. That stuff is behind us, whether we like it or not."

PJ nodded silently. There were tears burning behind her own eyes now. She couldn't remember the last time she'd cried in front of her brother—if ever. Her mom had instilled in her the need to be silent about her curse; it was physical in its intensity. Even now, she couldn't bring herself to say the unspeakable. How was she going to help Nanci if she couldn't even bring herself to talk directly about her own problem? This camping trip had to cover a lot of distance between her and Robert, and between her and herself.

"Robert. . . "

He stared at her. Their eyes locked.

PJ swallowed heavily. "Did you see her change?"

Robert's sharp intake of breath startled PJ. She felt cold adrenaline pour down her neck, and her scalp tingled. The fight-or-flight instinct in humans was stupid, she thought. The last thing she was going to do was slug Robert, although she did feel like fleeing from the truck, screaming and waving her arms around. But she'd have to come back if she did that, come back and face her destiny. She'd have to struggle with it, like Robert was struggling with it. A flash through PJ's mind made her realize Robert had been living with his worst fears for twelve years—the fear his child was a monster, and there would be no denying it when he finally saw it. PJ also recalled how he had to take a lie detector test every year. She wondered how deep the questioning got and if this was going to be an issue on Monday when he went to Indy for his test.

Robert was taking deep breaths. It had been nearly two minutes since PJ's question, and he finally answered.

"I tried to stay up last night. She was still a girl at midnight, three a.m., and five a.m. But, you know, I had to be in bed sometimes so Didi doesn't get wind of this."

"She doesn't know? Nanci didn't tell her?"

"No."

"Did you tell Nanci not to?"

Robert's lips pressed into a thin slit. Then he said, "Yes. You think that was wrong?"

The bell rang. Shortly, students started emerging from the building and congregating around the schoolyard.

"No, actually I think the fewer people involved, the better for Nanci. Whatever happens, she has a normal life, and we can help her keep it."

He exhaled heavily through an open mouth, and in his eyes, PJ saw distinct gratitude. "That's what I'm hoping for. More than I can hope for."

"It'll be okay, Robert, whatever is happening or not happening. She's normal, and she'll be fine. Even the freaky Peeping Jane photo-psychic has something like a satisfying life, with friends and everything. So let's figure this out."

"Tonight we'll both watch her. You know, normally surveillance is done with two people minimum. One has to keep their eyes on the subject at all times, every second, and the other one keeps notes, tells jokes, or does whatever is necessary to keep the watcher awake, fed, and entertained."

They saw Nanci emerge from the school doors and come toward them.

"Don't worry, Robert," PJ said. "We have the whole weekend. We'll figure it out."

* * *

The weather was perfect. They set up their two-chambered tent under a bright blue sky on a bed of pine needles and packed earth in the shelter of many budding trees. They moved the site's picnic table into the mesh vestibule of the tent and hung a lantern so they had a serviceable dining room as well as a spacious bedroom with three fat air mattresses. By six, they were seated around a roaring campfire. Nanci was reading a Nancy Drew book, Robert was checking his messages on his tablet, and PJ was sitting comfortably and staring at the sky above the treetops. It would have been an idyllic family campout, save for the fact the sun was slowly but steadily dipping on the horizon. PJ figured she had two hours before her change. She didn't quite know what to expect. She wasn't going to do it in front of Nanci, and she wondered how they would react to her afterward, when she was a black tabby. Would they smack her with a broom and shoo her away? She hoped not because she was looking forward to helping Robert with his surveillance. He could watch Nanci, and she would be entertainment.

For dinner, Robert cooked steaks he pulled from a cooler in the back of his truck. They had salad with the steaks and apple pie with partially melted ice cream for dessert. Nanci said it was the best day ever and the best meal ever.

Just after eight, PJ said she had to go.

"Go?" Nanci asked. "Where? It's getting dark soon. Are you scared?"

One of the excuses for their camping trip involved PJ's well-known phobia of the dark. They had told Nanci and Didi that PJ would be taking a long walk in the woods at sundown, sort of an exposure therapy, since being alone in the woods in the dark was the scariest thing anyone with PJ's affliction could imagine. In reality, of course, PJ couldn't be less afraid. As a cat, she felt she owned the darkness, being more comfortable and having better eyesight than mono-modal humans.

"Nanci, remember we talked about this?" PJ said. "Remember we said that if you can't handle something, sometimes the best thing is to just dive in the deep end and see how it goes? But you and your dad will be close by if I really need help."

"Okay." Nanci returned to her book.

"I'll see you off," Robert said.

"Are you sure you want to do that?"

He was pale, deathly pale, in the fading light with shadows from the firelight dancing over his face.

"Yes, I'm sure."

"Okay."

Robert turned to Nanci. "I'll be back shortly, honey. You going to be okay here?"

"Yuh-huh." She didn't lift her head from her book.

PJ and Robert walked into the woods, far enough that they were obscured to Nanci, but close enough to hear her if she called. Robert stood next to a large tree, facing the way they had come with his back to her.

"I'll watch Nanci," he said. "You...do whatever it is you do."

"It just happens. I don't need to do anything."

"Okay."

They still weren't talking about PJ's shift in anything other than vague allusions, which was fine with her. She was ecstatic at the possibility she would no longer be alone with her knowledge, but a lifetime of avoiding contact had made her unable to fully face the idea an ordinary human might venture into her world. She couldn't even begin to comprehend how life would be if there were another of her, if Nanci really was going to make the transformation too.

PJ watched Robert lean against the tree trunk with his arms folded across his chest. Her beautiful niece was in the lawn chair with her legs crossed and her foot dancing up and down as she read. World War Z could have broken out down the gravel road and Nanci wouldn't have noticed.

At eight-forty, PJ rubbed against Robert's calves. He jumped, almost treading on her.

"PJ?"

Yes, it's me, PJ said, but it came out as three unintelligible meows.

Robert stared at her. After a moment he reached down and stroked her soft fur.

"I don't believe it. This is not happening. How do I know you're not just a normal cat and my sister took off and is hiding somewhere? That this is all just an elaborate plot to make me look like a complete fool?"

"Rawr," said the cat.

"Okay, PJ, if it is you, we need some semaphores."

"Rawr?"

"A code. How about, one meow for yes, and two meows for no."

"Meow."

"Is my hair brown?"

"Meow."

"Are my eyes blue?"

"Meow meow."

"Okay, great. I really don't believe this. I'm talking with a cat."

He rubbed his sweaty palms on his jeans. PJ headed toward the campsite. Robert followed. When they got there, they saw Nanci had taken up a flashlight so she could see her book better. PJ rubbed against Nanci's ankle. Nanci's bobbing foot almost smacked PJ, so the cat moved away and jumped into PJ's chair. She settled into a ball and stared at Nanci.

Robert chuckled. "Nanci, did you see the cat?"

"What?" Nanci looked up at her dad.

He pointed at PJ, resting in the chair next to her.

"Oh! A kitty!" Nanci jumped up, leaving her book in her chair, all but forgotten. "Oh, you are a pretty kitty, aren't you?"

Nanci petted PJ for nearly ten minutes while Robert cleaned up their dinner mess, washed dishes, and repacked all the remaining food in the vehicle. When he came back to the fire, it was dark all around, and PJ was sitting in Nanci's lap, getting her ears gently scratched. PJ was purring for all she was worth.

"This is the most freaky thing I could ever imagine," Robert muttered.

"What?" Nanci said. "She's a cute little kitty. Who do you think she belongs to?"

"I think she's theirs." Robert waved his hand vaguely in the direction of a camper at a site in the distance.

"Well, she sure is a friendly little thing. And she can stay with us as long as she wants, right, kitty?" Nanci pressed her forehead to PJ's. "She doesn't have a collar. Maybe she's a stray."

"Oh, that reminds me. PJ—uh, I mean, kitty—can you come with me for a sec?"

The cat jumped from Nanci's lap and followed Robert to his truck.

"Meow?"

"I got you something." He opened the passenger door and reached into the glove compartment. He took out a small box. "Here."

PJ looked at the box.

"Oh, right," Robert said. "You don't have hands, do you?"

"Meow meow."

Robert chuckled. He opened the box and pulled out an exquisite collar of velvet and jewels, all colors of the rainbow. It looked vastly expensive. He slid it over PJ's ears onto her lithe neck.

"Careful, now. It's not a breakaway collar. But maybe we can cut it at some point and put a breaker in."

"Meow."

PJ groomed herself and purred loudly.

"It was our mother's, you know. I never thought about why she had such a thing. I just thought it was a big bracelet. But I know better now. And you know too, right?"

"Meow."

"All those years I grew up with her and never noticed. Crazy, huh?"

"Meow meow."

Robert laughed. "Come on. It's almost time to put Nanci to bed."

* * *

At nine, Robert put Nanci to bed. Although it wasn't a school night, they didn't want Nanci's sleep schedule to get out of whack. Nanci was twelve and more than capable of reading anything she desired—at a university level no less. PJ knew her niece still loved to hear Robert's sonorous voice read Nancy Drew, something the girl had grown up with and probably felt like she'd never outgrow.

"When I'm in college, you'll have to come over every night and read to me, Dad."

"Interesting idea. I bet by then you'll want me to stay as far away from you as possible."

"Why do adults keep saying stuff like that? I can't imagine ever wanting to leave you guys."

PJ curled up next to Nanci for the reading. They'd made it to the last two chapters in the book. Robert read one, then stopped. Both cat and girl yowled and yowled until he agreed to read the last chapter of *The Secret of the Old Clock* to them. In his soothing baritone he read, and both girl and cat were soon fast asleep before they learned the clock's final secret.

Robert poked PJ, and she awoke with a start. She realized it would be very difficult for her to stay up all night, especially since cat naps came so easily to her. Robert beckoned her from the tent. They left the inner flap open so they could see Nanci sleeping through the vestibule. PJ sat at the tent entrance. Robert sat in his lawn chair, reached into his vest pocket, and pulled out a pipe. He packed it with fragrant tobacco and lit it. PJ watched, yellow eyes wide and all-seeing. Fragrant smoke curled toward her, the scent of earthy tobacco mixed with charcoal. PJ had no idea he enjoyed a pipe. She suddenly felt like there must be a ton of things about her brother she didn't know. Already he was surprising her with his warmth and flexibility.

She came over to him and rubbed at his ankles. He stroked her back. "Nanci still asleep in there?" he said.

"Meow."

"Good. I think we can keep an eye on her from the vestibule. I brought a chess board. Do you think you can still play as a cat?"

"Meow."

After Robert finished his pipe, he set up the chessboard on the picnic table in the vestibule. PJ lay at the black end, and he sat at the white. He opened with his kingside pawn and she responded symmetrically. She had him trapped quickly in their first two games with daring gambits, and those games ended precipitously. PJ was learning she had to pace herself so the games lasted a while and had a chance to engage them to keep them up all night. At ten o'clock, Nanci was still a girl. A beautiful, fragile, slumbering, non-feline girl.

Around four, the night was at its darkest, and Robert was on his third cup of coffee. The fire was nothing but quiet, dark embers, and they were on their fourth game, PJ having won three. She liked to think she'd let him win the last game, to keep his interest and entice him to keep playing.

PJ's tummy grumbled furiously. Robert had been feeding her cat treats and tossed her another. She gobbled it up.

"You need water or something?"

"Meow meow."

"Okay. Well, let's set up the board and play again. I have a feeling my luck is changing."

* * *

The next day was very laid back. Nanci reread the ending about the old clock and started on another book she'd brought. PJ and Robert napped alternately. In the early afternoon, the three of them went on a hike. They passed a creek with pretty rapids and marveled at how quickly the trees were gaining their foliage. Early flowers in a grass bed shone under the sun in a wide field. At one point, Nanci pointed to a rock outcropping.

"Look! It's a cat."

There was a rock standing on its side that seemed to come to a point, like a feline ear. If you used a little imagination, the rock could have bespoken a cat.

PJ smiled. Robert said, "Okay, we can call this cat point. I think we're about halfway, so we'll be back in plenty of time for dinner."

That evening they had barbecued chicken and leftover salad and apple pie. Afterward, PJ announced she was going for her walk.

"Have fun. Is it helping?" Nanci asked, glancing up from her book.

"I think it is helping me."

"Well then, get going."

Robert laughed. "Nanci, don't be rude."

"Sorry."

PJ chuckled. She nodded at Robert and headed off to the forest. It wasn't long before she returned in feline form. She rubbed against Nanci's ankles, and the girl absentmindedly stroked her. PJ jumped into her chair and started cleaning herself. Her pink tongue darted out and caught her paw, and she rubbed her ear.

The idyllic scene was broken at nine when it was time for Nanci to go to bed. Then girl and cat curled up in Nanci's sleeping bag for Robert to read. He read for over half an hour and neither could resist his soothing voice so they both fell asleep.

When PJ came out around eleven, Robert was smoking his pipe. PJ came over and dared to jump in his lap. He stroked her fur, and she purred.

"I can't believe my sister can purr so loudly."

PJ closed her eyes, a gesture of trust, then opened them again and gazed fondly up at her brother. It wasn't long before the fragrant surroundings and comforting position had PJ asleep. She only woke up when Robert's pipe was extinguished and he moved to get up. She jumped down and followed him into the dining vestibule.

"More chess?" he asked.

"Rawr," she said.

They played until the moon was high above them. PJ found herself slipping into cat naps between moves, and her game was off. Robert won two out of three before she knew it.

"See?" Robert said. "I knew my luck had to improve. I still can't believe I'm playing chess with a cat. And losing at all. It's crazy."

PJ closed her eyes briefly and waggled her ears at him. He chuckled.

PJ was used to hearing night birds and buzzing insects, but at that moment, she heard another sound. It was a slight moaning from Nanci. PJ jumped from the table. She nosed into the sleeping area. Robert followed.

"What is it?" he whispered. "Did you hear something?"

Nanci was still sleeping, but there was a frown on her face. She complained softly and turned over. PJ's ears twitched and her nose quivered.

"What is it?"

PJ turned and bolted from the bedroom, through the vestibule, and out of the tent. She scampered behind it into the underbrush, sniffing the air and ground as she went. There was a familiar-scented animal somewhere close. A feline of some kind, which was odd since they were in the middle of the woods. PJ wondered if it was a wild cat or a domestic one.

Hello? Anyone out there?

There was no answer except for the chittering insects and calling night birds. The scent was fading fast. Whoever it was had left the area, PJ thought.

Then she heard murmuring from the tent. Nanci was up and talking to Robert. PJ ran back around the front and through the two flaps into the bedroom.

". . . sure of it, Daddy."

"Rawr?"

"Kitty," Nanci said. "Come here." She held out her arms and PJ climbed into them. Nanci stroked PJ behind the ears.

Robert said, "Kitty, Nanci was just telling me she's sure she was just a cat. Did you see anyone out there?"

"Meow meow."

"I think that means no," Robert told Nanci.

Nanci nodded. "Well, whatever I felt is gone now. But I was right there in the woods, outside, in the grass near our tent sniffing around. It was so vivid. It had to be real."

"Do you think you can get back to sleep?" Robert asked.

"As long as kitty stays with me." Nanci yawned.

PJ obliged.

* * *

The next morning, PJ was still beside Nanci when she woke up to the plea-surable scent of brewing coffee. From the light, PJ figured it was after eight. She dressed quickly and joined her brother over a newly stoked fire. He was making eggs for breakfast.

"So what do you think?" he asked her.

"Well, it doesn't seem like she's turning into a cat. At least not yet."

"Not yet? What does that mean?"

"Well, it started when I hit puberty. I don't really remember how it happened. But it's possible I was dreaming I was a cat before the changes actually started happening."

"Now you're terrifying me. Do you think my girl is actually going to turn into a cat?"

"I don't know, Robert. I'm sorry."

He eyed PJ. "How on earth did Mom hide it from us so effectively? How do you hide it?"

"People see what they want to see. No one expects that it's possible to turn into a cat. So they believe whatever story I tell them because they can only comprehend the improbable over the impossible."

"That sounds like what Sherlock Holmes said. 'When you have elimi-nated the impossible, whatever remains, however improbable, must be the truth.' "

"Exactly. And people think from the outset that it is impossible I could be turning into a cat. So they even discount what they see with their own eyes." PJ looked at Robert meaningfully.

He flipped the eggs. "I don't think I could ever hide something like that from Didi. She's too sharp. But that's why you never got married, right? You figured you could hide it, but then you realized you probably couldn't."

PJ's shoulders drooped as she recalled how madly in love with Liam she had been and how she abandoned him at the altar rather than share her secret. "Yep."

"You know what that means, though?"

"That Dad knew too?"

"Yes. And he never said a word to us. And we never found out before it was too late. Crazy."

"Well, if it's any consolation, the fact you're facing this makes me optimistic about love again. If you can come around, there must be another man on the face of the planet with an open enough mind. I just have to find him and get him to marry me."

"I haven't accepted this, PJ. I'm still in denial. If anyone ever asks, it never happened. I absolutely was not losing at chess all night to a cat."

PJ grinned. "You mean like I never took a photo in my life? I just get them dropped in my inbox?"

"Exactly. Except that's an open secret. This is a closed one. Solely among you and me and possibly Nanci—the blood Taylors."

"Got it."

Robert slid the eggs onto two plates and carried them into the dining alcove. PJ followed and they ate.

"Back to business," Robert said after he'd finished.

"What's that?" PJ was still finishing her eggs. She sipped her coffee.

"I assume you were a cat when you saw the Greene-Tate confrontation."

"Yes."

"Which is why your story keeps changing and it sounds like you're lying half the time."

PJ sighed. "Yes."

"How much did you see?"

"Everything. Until I fell in the water near old Mrs. Norton's house where Chip washed up."

"You're sure he washed up there? It wasn't just his shoe?"

"I'm sure. He was there, plain as day."

"And your vision at night is even better than a human's, right?"

"Absolutely. If I say I saw something, it was there."

Robert ran his fingers through his hair. "How on earth are we going to convince Detective Tipton of what really happened? Furthermore, what on earth did happen? How did Chip get back in the water and end up washed down all the way to the bridge?"

PJ smiled. "I've been thinking about that. And I have an idea."

18

Ruse

Monday night, Robert met PJ and Mutt on the stoop of PJ's trailer. He was wearing a ball cap and dark clothes. PJ had her backup camera in her usual collar and was ready to go.

"I can't believe I let you talk me into this," Robert said.

"Rawr."

"Woof!"

"Shh," Robert shushed Mutt. Then Robert turned to PJ. "Does he understand you when you're a cat?"

"Meow."

"How about when you're a human again?"

"Meow meow."

"Interesting."

Robert looked around. No one other than PJ and Mutt seemed to be in the area. "All right," he said. "Showtime."

He walked around to the back of his truck and loaded a cloth dummy onto his back. It was one of the type used for instruction at the police academy. It was heavy, not as heavy as Robert himself, but probably roughly as heavy as a skinny old guy like Chip Greene. Or at least in the ballpark. Robert loaded it onto his back and followed the animals down the ravine to where the branches met over the creek behind the Norton house.

The plan was to leave the dummy about where Chip had been, then Robert would skedaddle. Mutt would bark to bring old Mrs. Norton out, and PJ would be up in a tree filming what happened. They were all hoping Mrs. Norton would repeat whatever she had done weeks previously, when PJ thought she found Chip Greene on the edge of her property.

Of course, even the best laid plans can go awry. Robert didn't see Mrs. Norton until she was practically on top of him. PJ tried to warn him, but she had the hose out and spraying before PJ could get a sound out.

"Ahh!"

Robert covered his face with his hands and ran for all he was worth. He dropped the dummy to the ground. It fell approximately where PJ had seen Chip. Mutt danced around Mrs. Norton barking, and she focused the water on him. He yelped and ran down the ravine, the opposite direction of Robert.

By the time PJ finally got herself up a tree and ensconced so she could film the scene, Mrs. Norton had turned the hose off. She looked at the dummy. A string of profanity floated up to where PJ was. Mrs. Norton tried to take the hose to the dummy, but the hose was at the end of its reach and didn't quite make it. She threw the hose down, leaving it running, and stomped back up the ravine to her house.

PJ was dejected. The dummy lay spread-eagle in the mud at the edge of the creek. The hose was running and making the mud muddier. And there was no sign of Mrs. Norton.

Crap, PJ thought. This isn't working. If we can't show old Mrs. Norton pushing the dummy back into the stream, this is all for nothing.

After a minute, PJ turned off her camera and came down from the tree. She went to the dummy and sniffed it. It smelled like starch and mud.

Suddenly, water splashed against her. She yelped and ran. Mrs. Norton was back and swearing a blue streak. PJ jumped to the nearest tree trunk and scaled it. Mrs. Norton sprayed her with the hose until she was out

of reach, high up in the trees branches. Then, Mrs. Norton turned her
attention to the dummy.

"Filth on my property!" she yelled.

She tried dragging the dummy by a leg, but it was too heavy for her.
Instead, she got down on her hands and knees in the mud and pushed
against the dummy's torso. Slowly but surely, the dummy turned over.
Mrs. Norton redoubled her efforts and managed to roll the dummy into
the stream. It lay against the water's bed, stuck between two stacks of
rocks. Mrs. Norton screeched in anger and screamed profanities for quite
a while. Then she went back and got the hose and aimed it as far as she
could. The spray barely reached the dummy.

"Why aren't you going away?" Mrs. Norton cried. "Like the man?"

High up in the tree, PJ was hoping the camera's tiny microphone had
caught that. She guessed she'd find out, but she'd have to wait until morning. What a mess she was—soaking wet and shaking like a leaf high up in
the tree. I hope this works, she thought, staring at the profanity-producing
woman far beneath her.

19

Suspect

Two days later, PJ was at the county seat in the sheriff's offices. She was there to convince Sheriff Denning to question old Mrs. Norton, whose given name was Constance. At first, the sheriff wouldn't even see her. But PJ was nothing if not persuasive and talked his secretary into chiding him about his reluctance. She was granted entrance into his inner sanctum.

"PJ Taylor. What the devil do you want with me?"

It wasn't a promising opening, PJ thought. "Sheriff, I know what happened to Chip Greene."

"He drowned."

PJ sighed. "Right. But Alex Tate had nothing to do with it."

"The courts agree with you, if the judge who sat at his bail hearing has anything to say about it. That's old news. Why are you really here?"

"I need you to take a look at something."

PJ slapped an eight-by-ten of Constance Norton pushing the dummy into the creek in front of the sheriff.

"What's this?" He picked up the picture. "Is that a dummy? Where is this? Where did you get this?"

"Sheriff, watch this footage with me." PJ handed him a thumb drive.

"Hell no, PJ. I'm not stupid. I'm not going to plug some random drive into my computer."

"Well, my laptop is in my car. If you let me go get it—"

"PJ, no. This interview is over."

"But—"

"Get your tail out of here before I arrest it."

PJ couldn't believe the sheriff was being so stubborn. She had thought they were friends. She had thought he had been coming around and warming to the "photo psychic" who had helped his department and the Mayhap authorities so often, not to mention the FBI and DA's office.

"Sheriff, why won't you listen to me? I'm telling you what happened. That night Chip washed up downstream, and Mrs. Norton pushed him back into the water so he drowned."

"Slander. Pure slander. If you think for one minute—"

A new voice, a stark, gravelly woman's voice, interrupted. "She's got a point, Curtis. Why won't you listen to her?"

Vicky stepped out of the file room adjacent to the sheriff's office. The door had been ajar, and apparently she had been listening the whole time.

"Deputy Donnerweise," Sheriff Denning said. "This is none of your concern."

"That's bull and you know it. Get your head out of your butt, my dear."

PJ held her breath. She hoped Vicky's insubordination didn't result in her friend getting into hot water with her boss and husband.

"Victoria—"

"Curtis, I know you. I know you're a fair man and as curious as a darned cat. You must want to know what really happened that night."

"You have no—"

"Plus, I make your dinners, Curtis J. Denning, and if you ever want your favorite chicken-fried pork chops again, you're gonna listen, and we're gonna check out this video."

Sheriff Curtis sighed heavily. He looked Vicky up and down. She was standing arms akimbo, clearly set in her ways. The sheriff turned to PJ and looked her in the eyes. He shook his head slowly and spoke with shades of exasperation and defeat plain in his voice.

"Women."

* * *

Sheriff Curtis wanted to do everything by the book. PJ couldn't tell if it was because he was trying to give Constance Norton the most benefit of the doubt as possible, or because he wanted no room for Constance to squeeze out of the noose PJ had prepared for her. They arranged an interview for the next day in one of Mayhap's police station interrogation rooms. Constance showed up with Doc Fred and a lawyer, Renee Milton of Milton and Daughters. PJ felt pessimistic. She knew she had a theory and scant evidence. Everything seemed to hinge on Constance confessing. If she held firm, PJ wasn't sure what her footage showed. An old woman getting angry at some refuse on her property? Spraying everything in sight with a garden hose? What kind of evidence was that?

PJ was particularly upset that Detective Jake Tipton would be running the interview. She had to stop protesting though because Sheriff Curtis had threatened to bar her from the viewing room.

"PJ, you're a bystander. You're lucky I'm allowing you to be here at all."

At 11:15 a.m., Jake, Constance, and Renee were set up in the interview room. It was about the same size as the room PJ had been questioned in, only this room had a large window along one wall, behind which stood PJ, Sheriff Curtis, Doc Fred, and Vicky. Robert had decided to stay out of it as much as possible, hoping his role in procuring the dummy for PJ to use didn't come to light.

Constance was in a flowery dress, and Renee was in a three-piece business suit in navy, with a straight skirt that ended just above her shapely knees. Jake was plain-clothed in a brown suit and green tie that favored his eyes. PJ took one look at him and had to blush. After all that—even him almost shooting Mutt—she still found him gorgeous. He had nodded only briefly to her before they went into their respective rooms. It wasn't an encouraging nod, thought PJ.

"Please state your name for the record," Jake said.

Constance leaned forward and said to the tabletop, "Constance Marie Norton. Mother of Fred Norton. Grandmother to—"

"Thank you, that's enough," Jake said.

Constance glared at him. Renee patted her arm and murmured something to her. It sounded like, "Just answer the detective's questions as briefly as possible, Constance."

"I am Detective Jake Tipton, and this interview is commencing at," he consulted his watch, "eleven twenty-three."

"I am Constance Norton, and I concur."

In the viewing room, PJ snickered. The sheriff warned her with a look.

"Sorry," she mumbled.

Doc Fred patted PJ gently on the shoulder. "She's not right, you know," he said softly.

"I know," PJ whispered. "I'm so sorry."

Doc Fred nodded. "If she did something, it has to come out. We don't believe in secrets. Especially if good people are hurt by them."

Jake started talking, and Sheriff Curtis cleared his throat. PJ and Doc Fred shut up.

"Mrs. Norton, where were you on the night of Saturday, March 21 between the hours of ten p.m. and one a.m.?"

"What's that, son?"

Jake repeated his question.

Constance turned to Renee. "How in the hell should a person be expected to remember where they were on some random date?"

Jake said, "It was Saturday, a bit over three weeks ago, Mrs. Norton."

"So?"

"It was the night Chip Greene drowned."

"Oh. I heard about that."

"What did you hear?"

Renee cleared her throat. "Don't lead my client, Detective."

Jake nodded.

Constance seemed lost in thought.

Everyone waited. After several moments, Jake said, "Mrs. Norton? Where were you the night Chip Greene drowned? Do you remember?"

"That night. The nights. I've been hosing off out there a lot recently. The dirt seems to keep coming back."

"Out where, Mrs. Norton? What dirt?"

Renee frowned.

"Behind the house," Constance said. "There's dirt out there that never seems to go away."

"In the ravine behind the house, is that what you're saying?"

"That man was there."

Jake sat forward. So did Renee.

"What man?" Jake said.

"He left something behind. A shoe?" Constance said. "I heard about it. Or maybe I read it in the paper. I couldn't get it because the hose don't reach that far."

Jake said, "You found a man behind your house? Or a shoe?"

Renee held up a hand. "Careful, Detective. Constance, don't answer that question."

"Why not? I found a man. So what? He was on my property. I got him off my property. That's all I done. It's not my fault his shoe was still there."

Simultaneously, Jake said, "You got Chip Greene off your property?" and Renee said, "Stop."

Constance and Jake looked at Renee. She said, "I'm stopping this interview right here. You're going to have to arrest her or let us go, Detective. You can ask questions through my office later."

Jake opened his folder and spun it around. PJ knew that inside was only one thing: the eight-by-ten of Constance pushing the dummy into the creek, cleaning the crime scene as she'd done again and again since that fateful night, like Lady Macbeth, who couldn't get the dirtiness of murder off her hands.

"That's me!" Constance said.

"Detective, stop. Now," Renee warned.

Constance said, "Shut up, Renee."

"No, Constance. You need to keep quiet now."

"No, I don't. You don't know me." Constance turned to Jake. "Make her leave. I don't want her here."

Jake said nothing.

Renee stood. "I'll be leaving, but not without my client. Come, Constance. Please come with me."

"No."

"Detective Tipton, surely you can see this woman is in no condition to be implicating herself. If you continue, I'll have everything thrown out."

Jake said, "She seems lucid to me, Ms. Milton. And she seems to be saying she rolled Chip Greene off her property into the water."

Constance pointed at Jake. "That's it. That's it exactly. That man had to leave my property. It's my property. I got to protect it, don't I?"

"Please stop talking," Renee said.

"That man was messing up my property."

Renee pointed at Jake. "All of this is inadmissible now."

"I don't think so," said Jake.

Doc Fred left the viewing room, followed by Sheriff Curtis, Vicky, and PJ. Doc Fred knocked on the interview room door. "I'm sorry, I've got to agree with Renee. We need to get her out of there."

Sheriff Curtis opened the interview room door. "Time to go, ma'am," he told Constance.

"No. I want to talk to the detective. Tell him my side."

Then Constance saw PJ. "You!" she said. "You with the yellow eyes. You look just like that cat. And the cat saw it all, she did. Saw the whole thing. She'll tell you why I did it too. To protect my property. I always have to protect my property from the darn cats and squirrels and dogs, and even men. They're all messing it up."

Sheriff Curtis and Jake looked at PJ, whose stomach clenched. No one said anything for a moment. Then Constance started speaking loudly, her conversation degenerating into crass profanity.

Renee and Doc Fred together cajoled Constance down the hall with them. She screamed swear words the whole way.

As Constance's voice died off down the hallway, Jake said to PJ, "What was she talking about? Were you there that night?"

"No comment," PJ said, wary of admitting anything to the detective.

Sheriff Curtis and Jake stared at PJ. "No comment?" Jake said. "That must be a first."

PJ sighed. "I think it should be pretty clear what happened. I don't have to tell you, do I?"

Sheriff Curtis said, "Constance Norton pushed Chip Greene back in the water. But I'm not sure there's a court in the land that will convict her. What a resolution—a forgetful old lady who might or might not have facilitated Greene's death. How are we supposed to be happy with this?"

That was something PJ couldn't answer.

Graveside

A week later, the sun dipped into the western sky, and PJ stood in the cemetary, casting a long shadow over Chip Greene's grave. The headstone was simple with just his name and dates carved into its stone surface. Around her, magnolias shed their petals so she was surrounded by a pink, fragrant rain of sorts. Behind her, she saw a moving shadow. It crossed the grass and grew until it was larger than hers. It belonged to a man she knew well, who now stood beside her.

"Hello, Robert," she said.

"PJ. How are you? You picked an interesting meeting place."

"I just wanted to pay my respects, now that the whole thing is more or less resolved. Did you hear they arraigned Constance Norton today?"

"Yes. But, PJ, I can't imagine she's going to jail. I bet they'll work out a deal where she goes to the locked ward of Sunset Gardens or something."

Sunset Gardens was Mayhap's premiere home for aging folks and included facilities for people with advancing dementia, as Constance had.

PJ shifted from foot to foot. "That's probably best. We'll never be a hundred percent sure she actually knew what she was doing when she murdered Chip Greene."

"You were right about the whole thing. How do you feel about that?"

"I'm glad Alex isn't under suspicion anymore, but I can't say I feel good about putting an old woman away, regardless of how cantankerous and unpleasant she is."

"I know what you mean."

"Do the sheriff and Jake still think I lied about everything?"

"I'm not sure they know what to think. Your investigation helped push them in the right direction eventually. But your story changed so often, and was so hesitant in places, that I do think they still believe you made parts of it up."

"That's because the truth is so bizarre they would never believe it."

"You mean how you were a cat during the entire event?"

"Exactly."

"So what did happen? Tell me the whole thing. You don't have to leave anything out."

PJ briefly looked over her shoulder. They were alone in the cemetery. Still, she lowered her voice so it wouldn't carry on the tepid breeze.

"Well," she said, "most of what I told you was the truth. Only I wasn't at a distance with light goggles. I was right there with cat eyes, so I saw everything clearly. I filmed the entire thing, too."

"Where's the footage?"

"I'm getting to that."

"All right."

"Anyway, Alex was trying to sell Chip candy."

"Candy?"

"Every spring he sells candy bars for an autism foundation. For some reason, he had Chip cornered by the creek that night. Chip was accusing him of being behind the thefts in the trailer park, but Alex was just trying to sell him candy bars."

"That's interesting. None of that came out during the investigation."

"I know. I feel bad about that. Anyway, Chip grabbed Alex, who pushed him away like anyone would. Then Chip stumbled and landed in the water."

"What about the shot everyone heard?"

"I have a theory about that. It's just a theory, though."

Robert scratched his chin. "All right, go ahead."

"Mutt smelled the distinctive cigarette smoke of Sheldon Pike. I think he was there, probably with Trent, and I think Sheldon fired a shot from the same gun he chased me with."

Robert shuddered. "You're lucky you didn't get shot. It wouldn't take much to hurt a cat very badly, PJ."

"I'm fast and small. I'm a hard target to hit when I'm a cat."

"Even so."

PJ shrugged. "I have no evidence of that, but perhaps you could ask Sheldon about it."

Robert sighed. "I already did."

"You did? Why didn't you tell me?"

"You know I can't talk about open and active cases."

"Well, what did he say? Was he there? Did he shoot his gun?"

"PJ, I can't tell you. But let me just say your theory is very interesting, and I wouldn't worry about investigating further."

"So he was there, and he did shoot his gun."

"He's a trigger-happy boy, but you didn't hear that from me."

"Hear what?"

Robert smiled. "That's my girl. Back to Alex and Chip. What happened after Chip fell in the water?"

"Alex went in to try to rescue him. I have footage of them wrestling in the water."

"Why didn't you bring that forward?"

"Because it looks like it could go either way. From the context, I know Alex was trying to pull Chip out, and Chip was struggling against him. Then the shot sounded, surprising everyone. Alex dropped Chip, Chip started downstream, and Alex got sucked into the deeper water."

"I'm surprised Alex wasn't washed downstream as well. I guess Mutt had something to do with that?"

"I was calling and calling for Mutt. Finally, he showed up, and he went in the water and pulled Alex out. I chased Chip until he washed up on the bank near Constance Norton's house."

"I wish you could have called 911. It would have made a difference."

PJ swallowed. "You're telling me. I live with that guilt."

"It's not your fault you turn into a cat at night. And you weren't carrying a phone, right?"

"No, and I couldn't work one even if I was."

"After Chip washed up, did you see the old Norton woman roll him back into the water?"

"No. He was on the opposite bank. I tried to cross in the trees overhead but fell in the water. I was washed downstream, hit my head, and woke up the next morning with Bridget poking me. My camera was basically wrecked during the trip through the water. Only small snippets of footage survived, and they weren't much use."

Robert shook his head. He ran his fingers through his hair. "Jeez, PJ. We came that close to losing you. What a terrible thought."

"Yeah. It wasn't my best moment."

The two were silent for several minutes, contemplating the swaying foliage and dimming light around them.

"Does Jake still think you're the mastermind behind the Stoker Hills thefts?" Robert asked.

PJ snickered. "About that, no. He's dropped that line of thought."

"What's so funny?"

"Basically, I blackmailed him."

"You what?"

"Well, he doesn't have any evidence worth mentioning, and I told him a certain video would hit the light if he kept pursuing it."

"You mean the video you showed me of him being harassed by the squirrels and that little black cat?"

"That's the one."

"I'm amazed he dropped it. I would have thought something like that would have made him more stubborn to pursue you."

"I think the thought of everyone at the station and in the county seeing him the victim of squirrels and a kitten was too much to bear."

Robert laughed heartily. "That's funny. At least you're safe for now."

"Safe forever—Trent confessed. I guess he got a better deal confessing than when he was keeping his mouth shut."

"Good for him. Does it include jail time?"

"No. Some time in juvie hall, but mostly community service. A slap on the wrist, really."

"Well it's better than nothing."

"You know what I think?"

"What?"

"I think he turned state's evidence on his father's drug operation. That's why he's still walking around instead of being tried as an adult for bringing that package of ingredients to the cook house."

"Hm. Interesting theory."

"I know, Robert, you can't comment on open and active cases. You want to know what else I think?"

"I'm not sure if I do."

PJ was silent. She stared at Robert with her yellow cat-like eyes. He fidgeted under her stare and at last broke into chuckling. "All right, I do want to hear it. Try me."

"I think Sheldon Pike isn't in jail for either the thefts or the drugs because he's working for you."

Robert cleared his throat. "No comment."

"It's the only thing that makes sense. Otherwise, why wouldn't he have been arrested along with everyone else during the bust?"

"Who have you told about this theory, PJ?"

"Do you think I'm stupid? No one, of course. I know if he's one of your operatives, word of this could get him killed."

Robert nodded. "Just know that there are bigger and badder threats out there that we're working on, beyond Trent and Sheldon."

"I know." PJ patted her brother's shoulder. "But tell me," she said, "how did your lie detector test go? I completely forgot to ask you before."

"I failed."

PJ's mouth dropped open. "No."

"Yeah, I failed. On one question. They asked if I had knowledge of anything in general that would bear on the Bureau or my work for it. I said no. Of course that was a lie." He looked at PJ meaningfully.

"I guess your sister turning into a cat definitely has bearing on what the Bureau could do with it if they knew."

"You would make one killer operative."

"Well, I kind of am an operative," PJ said. "Just an informal, top-secret one with an odd talent."

Robert smiled. "Yes, I suppose you are."

"So what does that mean for your annual report? Are you going to get fired?" PJ sincerely hoped not. She often realized how many privileges she had with respect to law enforcement by having an FBI brother. She would hate to lose them.

"No, I'm okay. Everyone fails a test sooner or later. The quality of my work speaks for itself."

"Whew."

Robert eyed the setting sun. "When will you shift?"

PJ looked at her watch. "It's getting to be about that time. Want to watch me morph into a feline?"

"Part of me wants to watch. Part of me wants to run away screaming."

PJ felt the shift coming on. She turned to Robert. Her snout lengthened and her body started to shrink.

"Oh. Wow," he said.

After the metamorphosis, Robert stared at PJ for quite some time. She cleaned her face and paws carefully, then sniffed magnolia leaves. At last, Robert seemed to recover.

"Want a ride home?" he asked. "Or are you going to walk and explore?"

"Meow," PJ said.

"Does that mean you do want a ride home?"

"Meow."

"Want to play some more chess when we get to your trailer?"

"Meow."

"I can put the coffee on."

PJ started to purr and rubbed herself against Robert's legs. He reached down and picked her up carefully. She settled into his arms, and he stroked her back gently.

"Crazy," he said.

"Meow," she said.

They gave Chip Greene's headstone one last glance, then headed off toward Robert's truck in the direction of the setting sun. The sky was streaked with hot pink. PJ shifted in Robert's arms and said, "Rawr."

"I know. It's a beautiful sunset," Robert said. "Kind of restores your faith in life and the universe, doesn't it?"

PJ fully agreed.

Afterword

Thanks for reading! Please rate and review at http://www.amazon.com.
Look for more by Cy Wyss at http://www.cywywss.com. Sign up for Cy's
monthly newsletter and get a free short story!